LORD ILCHESTER'S INHERITANCE

When their mother and step-father both die of influenza, Sapphire Stanton and her two young brothers are evicted from their home. Discovering the existence of an elderly great-uncle, the siblings travel to his palatial residence of Canfield Hall, where they are welcomed with open arms. Then Sapphire discovers that their true guardian is actually a distant cousin — the arrogant but devastatingly handsome Lord Ilchester. Afraid of losing her new home and beloved great-uncle, yet irrevocably drawn to Ilchester, Sapphire must decide on her future, before others decide it for her . . .

FENELLA J. MILLER

LORD ILCHESTER'S INHERITANCE

Complete and Unabridged

LINFORD
Leicester

First published in Great Britain in 2015

First Linford Edition
published 2016

A catalogue record for this book is available
from the British Library.

ISBN 978–1–4448–2801–6

Published by
F. A. Thorpe (Publishing)
Anstey, Leicestershire

Set by Words & Graphics Ltd.
Anstey, Leicestershire
Printed and bound in Great Britain by
T. J. International Ltd., Padstow, Cornwall

This book is printed on acid-free paper

01490 9107

1

The journey had become wearisome and the twins, although good travellers on the whole, were becoming fractious after being cooped up in the antiquated carriage for two days. Sapphire tapped on the roof and the vehicle lumbered to a halt.

'Thomas, David, I believe we are no more than an hour or two from our destination; I think it would be perfectly in order for us to get out and walk for a bit in the countryside. What do you think?'

David, the older by the quarter of an hour, immediately spoke up. 'Can we have a picnic? Do we have anything in the hamper?'

'Indeed we do, my love. The landlady where we stayed overnight was instructed to pack it full of delicious treats as well as sandwiches. If you and your brother take a blanket, I shall bring the cushions and Jenny can carry the basket.' She threw open the door and kicked down the steps.

The coachman and under coachman, Ned and his son Billy, peered over the box. 'We can't stop here, Miss Stanton. Any vehicle coming around the corner will go straight into us.'

Her little brothers were already scampering across the nearby meadow, tossing their rugs into the air with glee. 'Hurry up, Jenny — pass me the hamper, and then we can allow the coach to continue without us. You will surely find a suitable place to wait, Ned, and we will catch up with you in an hour or two. As long as we arrive before supper there is no urgency.'

He touched his cap, flicked his whip, and the two sturdy bays ambled off down the lane. Sapphire hoped she had not made a foolish decision in stopping here without male protection. They were in the middle of nowhere, at least ten miles from the last village and a further five to the next.

Too late to repine; the deed was done. Now she was alone in a meadow with only her four-year-old half-brothers and maid for company. The field was brimming with wildflowers, scarlet poppies, blue cornflowers and golden buttercups bursting through the lush green grass.

Only then did it occur to her that there might be livestock in the field — something she should have checked before allowing her brothers to rush off like that. Then she realised her fears were misplaced — if there was no fence or hedge around the pasture then it was obviously not used for grazing.

'Jenny, shall we eat our picnic under this tree? If you would be kind enough to set the food out I shall round up the boys and the blankets.' She dropped the armful of cushions and went to call her brothers. They came at once, dragging their burdens behind them. 'Put the rugs under the tree, boys, and then we shall sit down. There is ginger beer to drink, which I know is a great favourite of yours.'

By the time they had munched their way through half the contents of the hamper, her brothers were ready to go in search of the carriage. However, they abandoned their blankets, leaving her to carry them as well as the cushions. 'We must walk in single file, boys, just in case a vehicle comes around the corner. I'm sure Ned will not be too far away.'

Her brothers scampered off, larking about and laughing as if they had no cares in the world. It was hard to credit that her dear mama and step-father had only been dead a few months. Her parents had been visiting friends when influenza had swept through the house, leaving few survivors. Sapphire had become the main carer for her brothers, as there had been no funds to employ a nanny or nursemaid, and they had scarcely noticed the absence of their parents.

Her step-papa, unlike the dashing Captain Stanton, had been a quiet, studious gentleman. She had become very fond of him and would miss his gentle humour as much as she would miss her dearest mother. Fortunately Sapphire had eventually discovered, when packing paperwork before being evicted from the family home, that they had a great-uncle, a bachelor of seventy years, who was now their only living relative and must therefore be guardian to the boys and herself.

The house they had dwelt in was rented, the furniture not worth keeping; so with the family's three members of staff, their two carriage horses and ancient travelling coach, Sapphire had set out for Hertfordshire without contacting her ancient uncle. She had no intention of allowing him the opportunity to refuse to take them in.

Tom shouted back, 'I can see them — they are waiting for us. Can we run ahead now, Saffy?'

'Yes, and tell Ned to be ready to depart as soon as Jenny and I get there.'

Jenny, no longer young, was puffing

and panting beside her. 'I'll be right glad to put this basket down, miss. Even half-full it's a bit heavy.'

Immediately contrite that she had allowed Jenny, as much a friend as a servant, to carry the burden alone, Sapphire dropped back. 'Allow me to take one of the handles, Jenny. I can carry the rugs and cushions as well.'

'No, I'll manage. There, I can see the carriage now. I reckon the horses will be well rested and will get on a bit faster now. How much further is it to Canfield Hall?'

'The landlady said it was no more than three miles from the village of Canfield, and that is the next place we get to. We shall be there long before dusk, Jenny; plenty of time to unload the trunks before dark.'

They trudged along in silence for a few yards. 'I wish you had written to Mr Bishop, miss. What if he is away from home?'

'He is an elderly gentleman and this is April. I must assume that he will, like most sensible people, wish to remain in the country during the spring.' She could now see the carriage for herself; it was neatly parked on a grassy triangle at the side of the crossroads leaving ample room for passing vehicles.

The boys were skipping about, talking non-stop to Ned and his son, and Sapphire prayed she had not made a catastrophic error by uprooting them without having secured a new home before doing so. 'Here we are, boys. What is all the excitement about?'

David hopped from one foot to the other, his blond curls flopping endearingly across his forehead. 'Ned spoke to a gentleman who rode by and he told him that Canfield Hall is the biggest, largest house anywhere.'

'That is good news indeed, David. It would seem that our new home will be far grander than our last.' She turned to Ned, whose normally glum features were almost happy. 'Did you by any chance ascertain how many more miles we have to travel today?'

He nodded vigorously, dislodging his cap and exposing his bald pate to the bright sunshine. 'The village is no more than a mile down that lane, Miss Stanton, and Mr Bishop owns all the land from here on.'

'How exciting! Mama could have had no idea she had such a wealthy uncle, or she would have applied to him for financial aid. Jump into the carriage, children, I am as eager as you to see our new abode.'

She watched out of the open window with more interest than before and could not help but notice that the cottages they passed, if not exactly dilapidated, could certainly do with some renewals and repairs. However, the people they passed seemed cheerful enough, and several village children waved to her brothers, who were each hanging out of a window. Tom was at her side and David with Jenny.

'Look, Saffy, there's huge gates and we're going to turn through them. Are we going to live in a palace?' Tom was bouncing up and down and David was equally excited.

'Not a palace, darling, but a very big house indeed. After all, Uncle John's home is called Canfield Hall and the village bears the same name. Now, I want both of you to sit down and listen to me carefully.'

Obediently they subsided onto the squabs and waited, no doubt expecting her to exhort them to be on their best behaviour or some such thing. 'Uncle John is not aware that we are coming to live with him, so do not expect him to be overjoyed to see us. However, he will not turn us away and, as we are such a charming family, I am sure he will soon be pleased that we are here.'

The boys exchanged a worried glance and then Tom piped up. 'Will he be cross and grumpy and make us sleep in the fireplace?'

Before she could answer this, his brother elbowed him in the ribs. 'No, silly, you're thinking of Cinderella.' David smiled sunnily; he was always the more optimistic of the two. 'He will be ever so pleased to have us living with him. He must be lonely by himself in that huge house.'

'Exactly so, my love; nobody likes to be on their own. Now, boys, let Jenny and me make sure you are respectable.'

After a considerable amount of bouncing and jolting, the carriage stopped in the turning circle. Somehow she was not surprised that their arrival prompted no reaction from those living in this magnificent, if neglected, house.

Billy appeared at the door and opened it with a flourish, then let down the steps. 'Shall I start unloading the trunks or go and knock on the door? I don't reckon anyone is going to come out to greet us.'

Sapphire was undecided — would it be presumptuous or sensible to arrive on the doorstep of her great-uncle with her baggage at her feet? 'Start unloading please, Billy. When everything is down then, Ned, I wish you to take the carriage round to the stables. Even if we cannot remain here permanently, the horses are far too fatigued to go anywhere else today.'

Her brothers arrived at her side and for once remained quiet. Jenny climbed down behind them. 'Best stop here, Miss Stanton. I'll go and bang on the door. There must be some inside staff and they can come out and collect our trunks.' Without waiting for her to confirm she wished Jenny to do this, her maid hurried off.

David tugged at her skirt. 'Why are the shutters closed, Saffy? Do you think Uncle John has gone away?'

'Perhaps he is dead,' Tom said dolefully.

'I am sure he is perfectly well, Tom. See, there are unshuttered windows at the far end of the building. I expect the others are closed inside the chambers that are no longer in use. Anyway, we shall be inside momentarily and able to see for ourselves.'

With a twin on either side of her, she marched across the sadly neglected turning circle and up the scrubbed marble steps. The door remained shut. The sound of the carriage wheels crunching on the stones caused her to glance over her shoulder. Good — if the carriage had gone then she could not be sent packing.

'Jenny, knock again and do it with more vigour.'

Her maid grinned, raised the dolphin-shaped knocker and hammered loudly. The boys giggled and this lightened the mood. 'They would have to be deaf not to have heard that, Miss Stanton.'

Tom pressed his ear against the peeling paintwork. 'I can hear someone coming.' He looked over his shoulder nervously. 'I can hear lots of people coming.'

He scampered back, and with his brother hid behind her skirts, Jenny was prepared to face whoever was approaching; but Sapphire shook her head.

'Come and stand behind me. Whoever it is, is less likely to be unpleasant if they are faced by me.' Although there had been little money to purchase new garments Jenny was an excellent seamstress and had kept the family well-dressed. There had been two trunks of exotic materials at her disposal which Papa had brought back with him from India.

Sapphire checked that her smart travelling gown was hanging smoothly, that there was no grime on her kid half-boots, and that her matching green bonnet was securely tied. She was glad at this moment that she was a statuesque young lady; had she been a diminutive blonde she would be quaking in her boots.

She had half-expected the door to be flung open and that she would be faced by a row of disapproving faces. However, there was the sound of bolts being drawn back and keys being turned before the door slowly moved to reveal three ancient retainers who appeared pleased to see them.

The least decrepit of the three, a gentleman of sixty years or more, stepped forward and bowed politely. 'I beg your pardon, miss, for the delay. We only use the rear of the house nowadays, and nobody has called at the front since Lord Ilchester's man came last year.'

'I am Miss Stanton and these are my brothers. Mr Bishop is our great-uncle and we have come to live with him.'

'My word, the master will be thrilled to have you here. Come in; Curtis and Smith will fetch in your trunks. I am afraid we have no chambers prepared, but Mrs Banks, the housekeeper here, will find you something suitable.' He bowed again. 'I am Robinson, the butler.'

'My men will bring in my luggage when they have seen to the horses, thank you.' She feared carrying something as heavy as the trunks might be the death of the two old men.

The butler shook his head. 'Not a bit of it, Miss Stanton. It might take them a bit longer but they will get your belongings in safely, don't you worry.'

Curtis and Smith nodded and set off remarkably briskly to collect the waiting trunks.

'We would like to introduce ourselves to Mr Bishop. Is he quite well?'

'A bit low in spirits, miss, but not too bad, considering. He occupies an apartment on the ground floor. I shall take you there directly.'

Sapphire wasn't sure this was the best option. She was fairly certain that an elderly gentleman would much prefer to be forewarned. 'Perhaps it might be better to send word to his rooms that we would like to see him at his convenience.'

'Bless you, miss, he will already know you are here. His drawing room overlooks the drive. Come along; it is a fair trek as he resides at the far side of this establishment.' He pointed towards a passageway on the left of the vast black and white chequered vestibule. 'It is easy to get lost until you get to know your way around the place, so keep close.'

15

Tom clutched her hand. 'I don't like this house. It is dark and smelly.'

Before she could reassure him a small, round woman dressed in grey bombazine appeared from a different corridor and bustled towards them, a broad smile on her plump face. 'Well then, what do we have here? Two splendid young men come to liven up the house. Shall I put them in the nursery, Miss Stanton, or do you wish them to be close to you?'

How did the housekeeper already know her name? Sapphire smiled. 'I should prefer them to be close by, Mrs Banks, and my maid also. Once we are settled and my brothers familiar with their surroundings I might reconsider.'

'Very well, miss. I shall have chambers prepared for you immediately. Do you wish your men to live inside or outside?'

'If the accommodation is acceptable then they would prefer to be outside.'

'That's what I thought. If your maid would like to come with me she can oversee the unpacking whilst you are speaking to the master.' The house-keeper dipped and then rustled away.

Their guide had not waited and she was concerned she would be left behind. 'We must run, boys, and catch up with Mr Robinson, for we do not wish to be wandering about the place for weeks.'

As they raced down the spacious passageway, Tom and David began to enjoy the experience. 'I think we should carry a bell, Saffy. Then we can ring it if we get lost.'

'I think that is an excellent idea, Tom. I believe there are at least two in our luggage somewhere. There, just ahead — I can see the butler is waiting for us outside those double doors.'

They skidded to a halt on the uncarpeted floorboards. Instead of being shocked by their display, Mr Robinson greeted them with a smile. 'I've knocked on the door, so you can go straight in. The master's valet, Fullerton, is waiting to conduct you.'

He opened the doors with due ceremony and stood aside to allow them to enter. They were greeted by another elderly servant, but again one who appeared delighted to see them.

'Miss Stanton, and Masters Stanton, you are indeed welcome at Canfield Hall. I have not seen the master so animated in many a year. Would you care to come this way? He is in the drawing room.' The valet escorted them to the door and then vanished. Sapphire did not have time to correct his mistake: the boys were Palmers, not Stantons.

The carpet was threadbare, and the furniture and draperies old-fashioned, but the room was pristine, with not a scrap of dust to be seen anywhere. This was a good sign — lack of funds must account for the dilapidation, but obviously the housekeeper and her staff were diligent and thorough in their duties.

Despite the warm reception they had received, Sapphire's heart was thumping uncomfortably. She was glad to have a small hand in each of hers to give her the necessary courage to meet this elderly relative who would in future have control of their lives.

The drawing room was gloomy; no candles or lamps had been lit even though dusk was falling. This surely was another sign of pinched circumstances. She hesitated in the doorway and glanced around the cavernous room. For a moment she thought it empty, and then she spied a huddled figure sitting by the window.

'Welcome, welcome, my dears. I cannot tell you how delighted I am to have you come here. You have made the heart of an old man very happy.' His voice was surprisingly strong for an older gentleman who was obviously in failing health.

2

Sapphire was obliged to keep a firm hold on the boys as they lagged behind, unwilling to approach the shrivelled figure in the armchair.

'Thank you for your welcome, Uncle John. I am Sapphire Stanton and these are Thomas and David Palmer, my half-brothers. Mama was your niece.' She was now within arm's reach and ventured a glance down at her uncle.

'Would you oblige me by bringing up chairs, my dear? As you can see, I am unable to stand without assistance, and staring up at you will give me a crick in the neck.'

Immediately her brothers stepped forward. 'We'll do it, Uncle John. We are ever so strong, aren't we, Saffy?' David nudged his brother, who reluctantly edged a little closer. 'I am David and this is my younger brother Tom.'

'I am delighted to meet you, boys, and shall converse with your sister whilst you fetch the necessary seats.' He gestured vaguely to the far side of the room. 'I think you will find what you want over there somewhere.'

Sapphire's brothers scampered off and she decided to sit on the window seat, although the cushion looked decidedly damp. She was about to settle when her uncle spoke again.

'Not on there; you will ruin your pretty ensemble. Could you come a little closer, my dear? I would like to examine the material more closely.'

'It is from India. My papa was there with the Duke of Wellington, of course; Wellesley had not been so ignobled at that time. Papa was able to ship back a trunk of wonderful silks and cottons.'

He stretched out a sticklike hand and gently ran his fingers across her skirt. 'I thought I recognised its provenance. I have an attic full of materials and artefacts I brought back with me. They have been mouldering up there these past thirty years and I hope you will make use of them.'

A hideous scraping alerted them to the arrival of one of the chairs. Sapphire was about to remonstrate with her brothers and tell them to pick the chair up and not drag it across the boards, but her uncle shook his head.

'Let them be, my dear. I care not for any damage they might do. No doubt you have already noticed that this magnificent house is in a sad state of repair. You might have surmised that a lack of funds is the cause, but I have more money than I could spend in one hundred lifetimes. It is ennui that is to blame. I have neither the inclination nor the energy to rectify matters.'

Tom and David arrived, red-faced and triumphant, with a chair each. 'Here you are, Saffy. You can sit on one of these and we will share the other,' Tom said.

'Thank you, boys. Shall we position them so Uncle John can see us without difficulty?'

After a further few moments of shifting and banging, the seats were satisfactorily placed. Sapphire smoothed out the rear of her gown and sat down, and her brothers followed suit. She hoped, for once, that they could sit close together without squabbling.

'I apologise for not informing you of our arrival, Uncle John. But as you are the head of our family and legal guardian of myself and my brothers, I thought it sensible to set off immediately when I knew of your whereabouts, and not delay matters by waiting for correspondence to be exchanged.'

He chuckled, a sound like corn husks rattling in a sack, and examined her closely. His eyes were the same deep sea-green as hers, while her brothers had eyes of blue like their own father.

'A *fait accompli*, my dear? I admire your spirit. I cannot think that many young ladies would have set off without knowing if they would be welcome on their arrival. However, you are under a misapprehension if you think that I am the head of the family.' He said no more and waited for her curiosity to overcome her good manners.

'I beg your pardon, sir, but I was under the impression that you are my only living relative, and therefore it is to you that we should apply for protection.'

'There is another who deserves that title: Lord Ilchester. We share a common bloodline. Our fathers were brothers, so I am his cousin. I am not surprised that you did not know this, as your mother was not privy to this information either.'

'I'm not sure that I understand exactly — are you saying that I should apply to Lord Ilchester and not yourself?' Her mind was whirling, trying to work out the exact connection between herself and this unknown aristocrat. 'So we are second cousins, or some such thing, to his lordship? If I am correct, then we share the same great-grandfather.'

'Exactly so, my dear. Lord Ilchester

and I are not friends, but he sends his man of business here once a year to see that I am still breathing. He believes himself in line to inherit my fortune when I kick the bucket. I cannot tell you how delighted I am that he will not now do so.

'My niece, your mama, eloped with your father and was cut off from the family. I was so disgusted at her treatment that I too left the familial home to make my fortune in India. I never heard from Susan again and had no idea that she had three wonderful children.' He cleared his throat and delved into his waistcoat to produce a voluminous white handkerchief. 'Unfortunately, my cousin must be considered head of the Bishop family.' Seeing her confusion, he added, 'He is Baron Ilchester, referred to as Lord Ilchester, but the family name is Bishop.'

'I have no wish to be anywhere but here with you, Uncle John. Could your cousin insist that I reside with him?'

'He is not famous for his hospitality

or generosity, my dear, so I expect he will be content to have you remain here.' His dry, rasping chuckle filled the space around them. 'However, he will be thrown all aback to discover he will not inherit my money.'

She could not help but smile herself. 'I believe that my brothers and I could be considered Lord Ilchester's inheritance — not at all what he will be expecting. Anyway, I have no wish to talk about your future demise. We have only just met and I am determined to become your favourite great-niece.'

'I never married and so have no close family apart from you and your brothers. My life has been devoid of interest and excitement for the past few years but with your arrival I am determined to remain alive for at least another ten years.'

'I am relieved to hear you say so, Uncle John, and I am equally determined to do what I can to make you happy. I only discovered your existence when rummaging through an old box of letters after my mother and step-father passed away some months ago. We must not repine, but rejoice that we have finally become acquainted.'

The boys were becoming restless; she recognised the danger signs. 'David, Tom, why don't you go on an adventure and explore this room? I'm hoping you will discover a bell to ring so that we might ask for refreshments. It is a long time since we ate our picnic.' They tumbled from the chair and dashed off, leaving her to talk to their uncle undisturbed. 'I apologise for the interruption. I hope you do not think me presumptuous.'

'This is to be your home now, my dear, and you must do whatever you want. I have a small and loyal staff, but like myself, they are past their prime. I shall hand over the running of the household and estate to you. You must do whatever you want to improve things, both inside and out. I shall set matters in hand first thing tomorrow.'

Tom raced back, followed by his

brother. 'We found the bell-strap and pulled it, Saffy. Shall we wait by the door?'

'Can we ask for cake when someone comes?' David said.

'Just tell whoever it is that we would like some refreshments brought here. We must leave it to Cook to send what she has available.' Sapphire turned to her uncle, who was watching this exchange with interest. 'What time do you dine? The boys usually have nursery tea and this is always served early.'

'I do not dine as such, my dear. My appetite is small and I usually just ask for a tray to be sent whenever the mood takes me. In future we will formalise things and eat at whatever time suits you.'

'I should like my brothers to eat at their usual time, if that is agreeable to you. I should like to eat as soon as they are settled for the night. I hope you do not wish me to dress for dinner?'

He shook his head. 'I scarcely dress

for the day, my dear girl, and have no intention of going through the bother of changing my raiment more than once in twenty-four hours.'

The door at the far side of the room opened and yet another elderly retainer stepped in. Immediately the boys explained what they wanted and the old man nodded and smiled. Without consulting her uncle or herself, he vanished, and the boys raced back, their boots loud on the uncarpeted boards.

'That was Dobson. He said that he is going to speak to the kitchen and trays will be sent at once,' Tom announced proudly.

David elbowed his brother out of the way. 'How can he speak to a kitchen? Kitchens don't have ears. You're stupid, Tom.'

'That'll be quite enough of that, thank you, children. You know perfectly well what Tom meant, David, so it is you who is being silly. You are supposed to be on your best behaviour and I am disappointed in both of you.'

Their faces collapsed and David's bottom lip quivered. Sapphire hated to correct the boys, but she wanted them to grow up with good manners and they no longer had parents to instil this in them.

'Now then, young man, don't look so miserable. I think your sister is feeling a bit crotchety. Perhaps she needs to go and have a lie down.' Uncle John winked at her and she hid her smile behind her hand.

David instantly recovered his *joie de vivre* and, forgetting his earlier nervousness at meeting his great-uncle, he moved to his side and then leaned trustingly against the old man's blanket-covered knees. 'We get sent to bed sometimes without supper, but Jenny always brings us up something later on.'

His brother joined him so the two boys were like bookends on either side of Uncle John's knees. 'Saffy doesn't have a room to go to yet, so she'd better stay here with us. I'm ever so hungry. I expect she is too.'

'I certainly am, Tom, and I have no intention of going anywhere until I have eaten my fill.' She looked around the room for a suitable table and spied what she needed in the gloom at the far side. 'I should like you both to help me move that table so the food can be set out on it when it arrives. I think we had also better bring another chair so we can all sit down to eat.'

By the time they had arranged everything to her satisfaction, the double doors opened and two parlour-maids, staggering under the weight of laden trays, were escorted in by Dobson. Sapphire was unsurprised to see that even the parlourmaids were well into their middle years.

'Thank you, this looks quite delicious. Please will you send my thanks to Cook and tell her that we will not require anything else tonight.'

The maids bobbed, but did no more than smile before leaving them to serve themselves. Obviously they stood on no ceremony here. 'Sit down, boys. Tuck your napkins into your collars and then I shall serve you. What would you like? We have pasties, a vegetable soup, cold cuts and pickles as well as fresh bread, butter and cheese. To follow there is fruit and what looks like an apple pie, plus slices of fruit cake.'

No sooner were the words spoken than she realised she should have offered to serve her uncle first, but it was too late to take this back. She smiled apologetically and gestured towards the food, but he shook his head, obviously in no rush to have his own meal.

Once her brothers were happily munching, she turned her attention to him. 'I am going to have a bowl of this delicious soup, followed by cold cuts, and bread and cheese. Would you like the same, Uncle John?'

'I shall have whatever you are having, my dear. I believe that for the first time in years I am hungry. Having somebody to eat with has restored my appetite somewhat.'

When they were all replete she gave the boys permission to get down and continue their exploration of the huge, sparsely furnished chamber. They wandered off, chatting and exclaiming, their demeanour and their prodigious appetite reassuring her they were content with their new abode.

'Do you think I should write to Lord Ilchester, Uncle John?'

'Not a bit of it, my dear girl. One of the outside men in my employ will no doubt pass on the information soon enough. When I come to think of it, I am overdue the annual visit. No doubt his minion will appear in due course and I shall be obliged to introduce you all.'

'If you will excuse me for a moment, I shall clear away the debris from our meal and then we can talk in comfort.' When this task was completed and she had shuffled the table out of the way, she resumed her seat and was ready to ask some pertinent questions.

'I think you should know that

although I have experience of running a household, I have no knowledge of how a place as large as this should work. Neither do I have any inkling of the management of so vast an estate. I think you must reconsider your generous notion to hand control of both over to me.'

He looked at her as if she were an escapee from the Bedlam Asylum. 'Good heavens, you have quite misunderstood my comments. I have no wish to burden you with such tedious details. What I would like you to do is just tell me how you think I could make things better here, and I shall put things in motion. That said, I'm quite certain you can manage this house without my interference. I might be in my dotage, my dear, but I'm well aware we are woefully understaffed and the house is desperately in need of renewal and refurbishment.' He sighed and brushed back a strand of his straggly grey hair. 'When I bought this place thirty-five years ago I was hopeful I would find myself a suitable bride and that she would take the house in hand. However, the young lady I had set my heart on married another and I never found anyone else I could contemplate spending my time with.'

Her eyes brimmed at his sad story. 'I am sorry to hear that you were disappointed in love, Uncle John. I can do nothing about that, but I promise you I shall do everything in my power to make your declining years happy and comfortable.' She gestured towards his legs. 'Forgive me for asking, but in what way are you incapacitated?'

'I suffered a seizure many years ago and it left me partially paralysed. The feeling in my left side returned eventually, but I believe my legs are too weak to support me anymore.'

'Do you not wish to be able to go outside, to walk about and play with the boys?'

His eyes flashed and she feared she had angered him. 'Of course I do. There is nothing I should like more.'

'In which case, Uncle John, we will work towards that end. I believe that when you are eating properly and have more to interest you, things will improve rapidly. In the meanwhile, however, I shall send for a bath chair so your valet can take you outside to enjoy the late spring sunshine.'

'I shall leave matters in your capable hands. Tomorrow we shall start to restore this wonderful building and the estate.'

Sapphire jumped up and embraced him, shocked to find how frail he was beneath her touch. 'I care not about my surroundings. My priority is restoring you to good health.'

On that note they parted. She collected her brothers and they bowed politely and said their goodnights. There was a footman waiting outside to conduct them to their accommodation, which was fortunate as the house was so large that she would never have found her way.

Jenny was waiting eagerly to greet

her. 'We have fallen on our feet here, miss, and that's for sure. You wouldn't believe the size of the room I have — three times as big as the one I had before. I have unpacked your trunks with the help of a chambermaid, and another maid has done the same for the boys.'

'Thank you, Jenny, for all your help today and yesterday. You must go and eat your supper now; I shall not require you again this evening. I shall put the boys to bed myself and then I shall retire. Although I am delighted to be here, I do wish we had known about Mr Bishop before now and so could have been part of his life for longer.'

'From what I've heard, Mr Bishop is not long for this world. Such a shame; he is loved by his staff and is a generous employer.'

'I refuse to believe it, Jenny. He is certainly frighteningly frail, but now I'm here I'll ensure he's eating more and gets out into the fresh air. If I had been incarcerated in that gloomy room for years on end I too would sink into a decline.'

When she eventually slid between the sheets and settled down for the night, her head was not full of expectation and relief that she had found a wonderful home with a loving relative for herself and the boys. Instead, the spectre of Lord Ilchester arriving and demanding to take control of their lives kept her awake.

3

April, Ilchester Abbey

Gideon Frederick William Bishop, better known in the vicinity as Lord Ilchester, was attempting to make sense of the accounts his mother had presented him. He was tempted to hurl the book across the room and just pay the damned bills without comment. He dropped his head into his hands and wished he was anywhere but here, surrounded by the detritus of his dear mama's extravagance and the growing pile of unpaid invoices he was discovering in boxes and drawers in his departed father's study.

Being the oldest son, he had always known he would one day take over the family estates, but he had not thought the time would come so soon for him to step into his father's shoes and assume the title. His parent, a hardened drinker and heavy gambler, had broken his neck in a riding accident two months ago, leaving Gideon to pick up the pieces. His mother had seemed more relieved than devastated by her husband's death; and certainly his sisters, Emily and Elizabeth, and his younger brother, Henry, did not seem unduly saddened by their father's sudden departure. The girls had always been close to their father, so one would have expected them to be devastated by his sudden demise.

They had been more angry than upset, as their come-out had been postponed. Gideon wished his sisters were as beautiful on the inside as they were on the outside; that they were less like his deceased parent and more like their mama. They had been indulged and petted by his father since they were out of leading strings and he blamed this for their lack of character.

It would be good when he could discard his armband and his family could came out of black. He had decided that three months was more than sufficient to wear mourning clothes; and if anyone in the neighbourhood thought differently, he did not give a damn about that.

For all his faults his father had not gambled away the estates, nor had he neglected his duties as a landlord. The villages, farms and smaller properties were in good shape and, as far as he could see, it was just the household bills that had been neglected. It appeared that his mother let money trickle through her fingers like sand, and his father had indulged his sisters and given them whatever they desired. His brother, at thirteen years of age, was away at school. Henry had returned briefly, but had been eager to get back to his friends.

Gideon smiled as he remembered his time at the same prestigious school. He had also enjoyed his time there, finding the company of his peers more enjoyable than his own home. At least he did not have to rush into matrimony, as his younger brother was his heir, and a perfectly good one at that. He was eight-and-twenty; plenty of time to think about setting up his nursery when he had passed his third decade.

Eventually satisfied there was nothing urgent he had to do apart from get his man of business to settle the outstanding accounts, he pushed back his chair and strode to the window to survey the rolling parkland. Although the estates were prosperous, his parent had been seriously overspending and a retrenchment was necessary if they were not to fall into serious debt. Fortunately the grounds were well-maintained, the drive weed-free; and the Abbey, for all its great age, was in good fettle and required no urgent repairs or renewals.

A polite tap at the door dragged him from his reverie. He returned to his desk and called a brusque instruction to enter. Foster, the estate manager, stepped in, his cap in his hand. Gideon could not like the man — he had a shifty appearance — but had so far found no reason to doubt his probity.

'What can I do for you, Foster? I was about to go out.'

The man shuffled forward. 'I was wondering, my lord, if you wish me to make my annual visit to Canfield Hall.'

'Canfield Hall? Why should you wish to go there? What interest is this place to me?'

'Mr Bishop, the owner of the place, was cousin to your father, my lord. He is an elderly and infirm gentleman and you are now his closest relative. The previous Lord Ilchester sent me every year to make sure he was . . . well.'

The noticeable pause between the words registered with Gideon. What the man meant was that he was sent to see if Mr Bishop was still breathing. There was more to this than the wretched man was revealing.

'Thank you, Foster, but there is no need to concern yourself. I shall visit Canfield Hall myself in a month or two. I had no idea there was another branch to this family, and it is high time I discovered something about it.'

He flicked his hand and the man retreated. As soon as the door was closed, Gideon went in search of his mother. She might be an extravagant parent, but he was fond of her and his brother. He wished he felt the same about his sisters.

He found Emily and Elizabeth sitting with his mama in the garden room surrounded by yet more fashion plates and swatches of expensive materials. Neither girl got up to greet him. They were seventeen, Emily the oldest by a few minutes, and already both were beautiful. He would have to watch them carefully when they were presented to ensure they made no unsuitable connections.

'Have you finished your tedious paperwork, dear brother? We were hoping you would come with us to visit Lady Redmond when we make our morning calls.'

'I would rather have my teeth pulled,

Emily, but I send you out with my good wishes. Mama, it is you I have come to see. What can you tell me about a Mr Bishop of Canfield Hall?'

His mother, still a pretty woman although already in her middle age, smiled and patted the seat next to her. 'Darling boy, I cannot believe you did not know of him. He and your papa were at daggers drawn all their lives, but your father liked to keep an eye on him. He is as rich as Croesus; came back from India with more money than he could ever spend. And as he is unmarried, and has no other living relatives, you will understand why your father took such an avid interest in his well-being.'

Elizabeth overheard their conversation. 'Papa said we would have the biggest dowry in the land when Mr Bishop dies. He is very old and sick so hopefully that day will come soon.'

'Do not speak so disrespectfully, Elizabeth. I will not have it.'

Gideon's sister coloured. 'I beg your

pardon, Mama, but it was what Papa always said. And although *you* have the title, brother, *he* has the wealth in the family.'

Gideon shuddered. His sisters were more like their father than he was, and this was not to their advantage. They also had his colouring — blonde hair and grey eyes, whereas he and Henry resembled their mother, with dark hair and unusual sky-blue eyes. He decided to ignore her comments, as Mama would take her to task when he had gone.

'I wonder if he knows that there is a new Lord Ilchester. I should have enquired from Foster where Canfield Hall is situated. I don't suppose that you know, do you, Mama?'

'I do indeed, my love. It is no more than an hour or so across country — so your father told me. It would be perfectly possible for you to get there and back in the day.'

'Thank you, Mama. I am too busy here at present, but will ride over there in the summer and introduce myself. I wonder why he and my father were at loggerheads? It will be worth the ride just to discover that.'

He left the ladies of his family discussing the current fashions and deciding which ensembles they would order for the summer. He had already told them they must curtail their lavish spending. His inheritance was sound, and hopefully without the drain of his defunct parent's gambling and hellraising there should be more than enough to keep his sisters and mother fashionably attired.

He did not stint on his own apparel. His clothes were made for him at Weston's, as were his waistcoats and breeches. Although he was fond of his mother, he had made a point of remaining on his own estate — a substantial one no more than fifty miles away — whenever his father was in residence. He visited London in the Season, but never stayed at the family town house in Grosvenor square, instead taking lodgings in Albemarle Street.

As he strolled off to take his morning ride, he decided that Mr Bishop deserved more respect and consideration than the annual visit from the estate manager, who went solely to check that the old gentleman was still breathing.

★   ★   ★

The weeks passed; and the longer she lived in Canfield Hall and the better she got to know her uncle, the happier Sapphire was with her life. The doctor had pronounced himself amazed at the difference in his patient. Uncle John could now walk with only the aid of his silver-topped cane, although he did seem to enjoy being pushed about the place in his smart bath chair. A dozen extra indoor staff had been appointed, all of them young and fit, and the house had been cleaned and polished until it sparkled. A team of labourers were working their way around the chambers in the central part of the house, and Sapphire was sure that before the end of the summer every room would have been redecorated and refurbished.

She smiled at her small family with satisfaction as they sat around the table eating supper together. She had soon abandoned the idea of the boys having nursery tea and she and her uncle dining informally later on. Uncle John had insisted he wished to spend every available minute with his nephews and niece, and so matters had been arranged to accommodate these wishes.

'Are you excited about your anniversary, boys?' Sapphire asked them. 'I cannot believe you will be five years old tomorrow. It seems only yesterday you were still in leading strings.'

'I wish you would tell us what we are being given, Saffy. I shall just burst if I have to wait much longer.' David looked from one to the other with shining eyes.

'Birthday gifts must be given on a

birthday, young man,' said John. 'You will just have to contain your impatience. It will be your big sister's name day next month — you would not wish her to discover what we are giving her before that date, now would you?'

'No, Uncle John, we wouldn't. It is to be a very big surprise, Saffy, and you must not ask us anything about it.'

'I shall be twenty years of age, almost an old maid,' she said with a smile.

'What's an old maid, Saffy?' David asked.

'It is a young lady who has not found herself a husband,' said John, 'and it is fustian to refer to yourself as such, my dear girl. I have every intention of introducing you to my neighbours very soon, and you will have the pick of the county. You are a rich, beautiful and intelligent young lady, and I will be fighting off your suitors with a stick.'

The boys were delighted with this idea. 'Will you use that stick, Uncle, or a different one?' Tom said.

'If a lady who is not married is called an old maid, is Uncle John called an old lad?' David joined in.

'Now you are being very silly, both of you, and it's time for bed,' Sapphire told them. 'Meg is waiting for you by the door. Run along now, and I shall be up to tuck you in in an hour.' She waited until her brothers were safely out of earshot before turning back to her uncle, who was sitting rather smugly, sipping his claret.

'Uncle John, I have absolutely no intention of being paraded around the neighbourhood by you or anyone else. If the good Lord sees fit to send me someone I can fall in love with, so be it, but otherwise I am content as I am. And I can assure you, that even if I did meet a suitable gentleman and he reciprocated my feelings, then unless he was prepared to live here, nothing would ever come of it. I am not going to leave you.'

'But you do consent to inviting our neighbours to a garden party for your birthday, my dear? I have not entertained here for twenty years or more, and I would so enjoy a small gathering and to introduce my niece and nephews to local society.'

'In which case, I shall enjoy planning it with you. It would be wonderful to invite the locals as well — make it an annual event, perhaps? We could have stilt-walkers, fire-eaters, a Punch and Judy show for the children, and maybe dancing and fireworks.'

'Heavens above! You have the bit between your teeth and no mistake, my dear. Let us indeed have a garden party for everyone.' He laughed, and she was struck by the difference in the sound. His once pale, emaciated face now radiated good health and happiness. 'I had not thought of something quite so grand. However, you're right to wish to include my tenants and their families in our celebrations. My man of business can assist you, and the housekeeper and butler will want to be involved as well.'

'I wish now that we had arranged a

party for the boys. I hope they will not be disappointed with what we've planned.'

'Disappointed? I should think not, my girl. They have a pony each and a puppy to share — what more could two little boys desire? Then you are going to teach them to swim, and we shall have a picnic by the lake together.'

'We have accomplished so much since I got here, and apart from the lingering smell of paint and the constant sound of hammering, we have scarcely been inconvenienced at all by the workmen doing the redecorations and refurbishments.'

'I care not for such things, but am pleased to have Canfield Hall smart for your sake, my dear girl. However, I am thrilled to have young Jarvis to push me around in my magnificent bath chair. That was a stroke of genius. If I had thought of it myself I should never have gone into such a decline.'

'I think you are almost ready to abandon it, Uncle John, but I shall be sad to see it go. I have never laughed so much as when I've watched you and the boys being trundled about the place.'

He pushed himself to his feet, waving away her offer of assistance. 'I can manage perfectly well, thank you. The more I exercise my legs the stronger they will become, so the physician tells me. How are your driving lessons coming along? I'm not surprised that you are already an excellent horse-woman. Your mother was a bruising rider.'

'I am proficient with the pony and cart, and have now moved on to driving the barouche and the gig. Ned and Billy are thrilled to have charge of a stable full of prime horseflesh. Our two old carriage horses have been retired and are now living a life of luxury in the back pasture.'

'Do you like the little mare I got for you?'

'Starlight is everything one could wish for in a mount. Now, if you will forgive me, I must go up and read to the boys. I doubt they will sleep much tonight; they're far too excited.'

* * *

The next morning dawned as bright and sunny as the previous three weeks had been. Sapphire now had Jenny as her dresser and was beginning to enjoy the luxury of having her ensembles chosen for her. 'I shall be back to change into my swimming garment after the boys have seen their ponies and puppy, and I shall wear my new primrose muslin morning dress until then. I do not wish to wear more than one petticoat.'

'An excellent choice, miss. Yellow complements your lovely chestnut-coloured hair perfectly.' Jenny held out the item designed for swimming. 'I'm not sure this is quite decent, miss. When it is wet it will cling to your form in a most revealing way.'

Sapphire agreed. 'You are probably correct, but as there will be nobody to see me apart from my uncle and brothers it is of no matter.'

'What about the outside men? They will be gawping from somewhere behind the hedges.'

'Ned will make sure that doesn't happen — he is as concerned for my decency as you are.' Sapphire glanced quickly in the full-length mirror and was quite satisfied with her appearance. She too had gained weight, and no longer looked like a beanpole with a mass of russet curls. Even her eyes were brighter and more green than brown nowadays.

She had intended to collect her brothers on the way past, but she could hear them running about downstairs, and Uncle John was also up and about far earlier than usual. She rather thought breakfast would have to come after the visit to the stable yard.

'Happy birthday, David and Thomas. It is a spectacularly beautiful day today — perfect to celebrate with a picnic and a swim. Good morning, Uncle. I had not expected to see you just yet.'

'I am as eager as the boys to begin this day of celebrations. I think I should like a breath of fresh air before breaking my fast. Boys, would you be kind enough to fetch young Jarvis and my bath chair?'

Her siblings scampered off to return moments later. 'Can we climb in too? Having a ride with you is ever so good for a birthday treat,' David said eagerly.

'Absolutely right, young man. Now, allow me to get myself settled, and then you can scramble in between my legs.' He looked at his assistant. 'I think I should like to perambulate to the stable yard this morning. Are you feeling strong enough to push us over the cobbles?'

'Fighting fit, sir, and these little chaps weigh no more than a feather.'

The journey around to the stables was accompanied by shrieks of laughter, and at one point David toppled from the bath chair, much to his brother's amusement. Undeterred, he jumped to his feet and dived back on again.

Sapphire was surprised the boys hadn't realised there was a reason for their visit to the stables. When Jarvis pushed them through the archway even she was silenced. Standing side by side were two matching Exmoor ponies, immaculately turned out and with ribbons plaited through their manes and tails.

'Are these for us, Saffy? Our very own pony each?' Tom was out of the bath chair, closely followed by his brother, and was about to rush at the ponies.

'Quietly now, boys. You will startle them if you are too noisy and brash,' Uncle John said firmly.

Immediately they obeyed and waited to be given permission to advance. 'Come along, lads, let me introduce you to Merry and Bruno,' Ned said and beckoned them over.

When the puppy was brought out they were rendered speechless once again. Sapphire watched them with a full heart and thanked God for bringing her here. They decided to call the dog Silly, as he was indeed a little clown. They agreed that until he was house-trained he would remain outside.

By the time they had received their first riding lesson and returned to the house for a very belated breakfast, it was almost midday — time to go to the lake and change into their swimming suits in the boathouse. There were already tables and chairs set out under a handsome willow tree, plus rugs and cushions on the grass, as the brothers would be more comfortable eating their picnic there than sitting at a table.

Meg helped the boys change into their costumes and Jenny assisted Sapphire. With the pretty mob cap covering her hair and the pantaloons down to her ankles, she was fairly sure there was less of her on view than when she was dressed normally.

'I am ready now, boys,' she said. 'Are you?'

They appeared from behind the screen, giggling and shoving each other. They looked as ridiculous as she, and she felt they would have been better served to enter the lake in their birthday suits. She smiled at her thoughts and led the way to the steps at the end of the boathouse.

'Now, boys, you must listen very carefully to my instructions. The water at the edge comes only up to your waist, but if you move away from there you will be out of your depth. Whilst I am teaching one of you, the other must remain close to Meg and Jenny, who will be watching from the bank. Is that quite clear?'

They nodded solemnly. She took the hand of each child and together they stepped into the water. She had expected it to be cold, but it was surprisingly pleasant. David squeezed her hand.

'What if we want to . . . you know . . . relieve ourselves? Do we have to get out and go into the house?'

'I am sure nobody will notice if you do not, but I have no wish to be informed.'

They emerged into the bright sunlight and she gently steered David to the bank. 'As David is the eldest, I shall begin my instructions with him. Why don't you hold on to the bank and kick your legs, Tom?'

After forty riotous minutes, Sapphire had lost her cap and her hair had tumbled from its pins to hang in damp cascades around her shoulders. Both boys could now do a respectable distance in doggy-paddle, and she was confident that with a few further lessons they would be competent swimmers.

'I am going to swim to the centre of the lake whilst you play in the shallows,' Sapphire told them. She struck out strongly. As she reached the centre where the water was cool and deep, she turned and began to swim back, concentrating on keeping her stroke even and enjoying the sensation of ploughing through the water at speed.

When she reached the bank she stood up, shaking her head to clear the water from her eyes. To her horror, she saw that they were no longer alone.

4

Gideon enjoyed his cross-country ride to Canfield and was hopeful of arriving at the usual time for morning calls — that was, early afternoon. The directions he had received from his estate manager were exemplary and he had no difficulty finding his way.

The villages and farms he saw were in good repair, and he received many cheery waves from children as he cantered past. The sun was at its zenith and, despite wearing his lightest jacket, he was feeling decidedly warm. As he turned into the drive of Canfield Hall, he spied the shimmering water of an ornamental lake. This was a goodly distance from the house, but he decided nevertheless to make a short detour. The water looked too inviting to ignore.

It would be uncouth to ride across the immaculate grass, so he slowed his mount to a sedate walk. Only then did he spy a small group at the side of the lake adjacent to the well-kept boathouse. There seemed to be some sort of picnic going on as there was an array of tables, chairs, rugs and cushions on the grass. Amongst the group he saw two maidservants, a footman and a smart, grey-haired gentleman who was sitting on one of the chairs shouting encouragement to two small boys who were splashing and paddling in the water.

They had not heard Gideon approaching, so he dismounted and hooked his mount's reins over his arm before strolling towards them. He cleared his throat noisily and one of the girls almost toppled head first into the lake at the sound.

'I beg your pardon for intruding. I am Ilchester. I have come to introduce myself.'

The old gentleman got to his feet and walked with the aid of a cane towards him. 'Are you, by God? I take it your father has kicked the bucket?'

'He has. I thought I would come and

inform you myself. He broke his neck in a riding accident in February.' Gideon bowed, scarcely able to believe this sprightly person was Mr Bishop. 'You are Mr Bishop, I take it? I have been misinformed about your health, sir, and am delighted to find you looking so well.'

'Not as delighted as I am, my boy.' He gestured towards the two children perched round-eyed on the edge of the bank. 'These are my great-nephews, Masters David and Thomas Palmer, and today is their fifth name day.' He turned with a strange smile on his face. 'And this, my lord, is my great-niece, Miss Stanton.'

Gideon could not believe his eyes. Arising from the waters was Aphrodite herself — a beautiful young woman with cascading chestnut locks, her womanly curves intriguingly displayed beneath her sodden garment. He had never seen anything so lovely, or so desirable.

For an instant Sapphire remained

still, the shock of being ogled by this unknown gentleman rendering her immobile. Then common sense returned and she collapsed inelegantly, leaving only her head above the water. Who was this intruder? How dare he stand there with his blue eyes staring into her very soul?

She recovered sufficiently to speak. 'I do not care who you are, sir, but you are *de trop*. Only a nincompoop would think himself welcome at such an intimate family gathering. Kindly remove yourself at once.'

She had expected him to take exception to her appallingly rude remarks, but instead she watched a tide of crimson creep above his casually tied neckcloth until his entire face was an interesting shade of beetroot. Without saying a word, he turned and vaulted athletically onto his bay stallion and cantered across the lawn and off down the drive.

Only then was she aware that her uncle was laughing helplessly and Jenny and Meg were trying to hide their smiles behind their hands. Her siblings were looking bemused, as well they might.

'Who was that man? Why are you laughing, Uncle?' David asked.

Sapphire was not amused. Her uncle spluttered to a halt and mopped his streaming eyes. 'That, my dear girl, was Lord Ilchester come to pay his respects.'

Scalding heat travelled from her toes to the tips of her ears. He was the head of the family and she had sent him packing. Not only that, but she had embarrassed him, and it was hardly his fault that he had arrived at such an inopportune moment. Now she had time to think clearly, she realised he would not have seen her swimming until he arrived at the edge of the lake.

No, Lord Ilchester was not to blame; her uncle was the person responsible for her humiliation. 'I am most displeased with you, sir. You should not have introduced me, and have warned me to remain beneath the lake.'

Not waiting to see his reaction to her reprimand, she scrambled nimbly from the water and ran to the boathouse. 'Boys, you must stay here and enjoy your treat, and I shall return in time for the picnic; I am going to try and undo the mischief your uncle has done.'

She tore off her wet garment and dragged her morning gown on over her wet body, and then with her slippers in one hand and her skirts in the other, she raced for the house. There were several interested spectators, but she ignored them. She must change into her riding habit and go after Lord Ilchester and make her apologies.

Robinson was hovering in the vestibule. 'Have my mare saddled immediately. I shall be going out in ten minutes.'

She found her clothes and was half-dressed when Jenny puffed in. 'Here, miss, let me put your hair up as it's making your clothes all wet.'

In slightly over the allotted time Sapphire was out of the house and in the stable yard, where her horse was waiting. Ned was ready to accompany her. 'No, Ned, I don't wish you to come with me.' He tossed her into the saddle and, from his expression, was not happy with her instruction but had the good sense not to argue. She had no wish for an audience when she accosted Lord Ilchester.

She trotted out of the yard and urged the mare into a canter, then clicked her tongue and was galloping down the drive with scant regard to safety or decorum.

★　★　★

Gideon had never been so embarrassed in his life. Miss Stanton had been perfectly within her rights to dismiss him so rudely. As soon as he had seen her swimming towards him he should have removed himself. Although young ladies took the waters in Bath, they did so without being stared at by fools like him.

He could not set off for home so

soon; his mount needed fodder and rest after his two-hour cross-country ride. He would head for the village in the hope there was a posting inn of some sort where he could seek refreshment for himself and his mount. He would write a grovelling letter of apology and hope to be invited to return.

There was no urgency, as his horse could walk the two miles whilst he enjoyed the countryside. After a few minutes he decided to dismount and let his horse graze on the lush grass that grew on the side of the lane. He propped himself against a sturdy farm gate and went through the embarrassing scenario in his head. Good grief! Mr Bishop had orchestrated the whole thing. He could have warned both of them, but he had deliberately set out to cause the maximum embarrassment.

Everything about today was a surprise. Mr Bishop was no more on his deathbed than he himself, and he certainly wasn't all alone in the world, as he had three young and healthy relatives.

Gideon had Sultan's reins looped loosely around his wrist when the animal threw his head up, tearing the leather from his grip. Before he could snatch them back his stallion half-reared and shot off in the direction of Canfield Hall.

He turned the air blue with his language and prepared to return to the scene of his humiliation. The lane had high hedges that curved, so he was unable to see ahead of him. The sound of approaching horses made him increase his pace. Someone had caught his errant stallion and was returning it to him. Then, to his shock, the one person in the world he wished to avoid arrived, leading Sultan.

'My lord, I hope you did not take a fall. You have been caused sufficient embarrassment for one day. I came after you in order to apologise.'

Miss Stanton leant from the saddle and handed him his reins. For some strange reason for a moment he was short of breath, unable to do more than nod. Then he recovered his aplomb and bowed.

'Thank you for bringing him back to me. Miss Stanton, you have no reason to apologise to me. I should have sent word that I was visiting today, and when I saw you in the lake I should have retreated immediately. I offer you my sincere and humble apologies.'

'In which case, my lord, shall we begin again?' She smiled and he was rocked once more by her beauty and charm.

He remounted and placed his horse beside hers. 'If you will forgive me for saying so, I believe the real culprit in this is Mr Bishop. Your great-uncle has a wicked sense of humour.'

'Indeed he does, and I shall forgive him eventually. We were about to have a picnic by the lake. Would you care to join us? If that is too informal for you, then we can remain indoors.'

'I should love to join you outside, but

before we do so there are one or two things I should like to ask you.'

She explained how she and her brothers came to be residing at Canfield Hall, but then hesitated as if she had something more serious to impart. 'My lord, my uncle seems to be of the opinion that, as head of the Bishop family, my brothers and I are now your wards. Even if this is the case, I want to make it perfectly clear I have no intention of living anywhere but at Canfield Hall. My brothers will inherit the house and the estate one day and they must learn how to become good landlords. They cannot do this living elsewhere.'

Until she pointed it out he had not considered this fact. The last thing he wanted was to inherit more responsibility; he had enough to cope with at home already. He shook his head. 'I suppose that might be the case in law, Miss Stanton, but I can assure you that as far as I'm concerned, Mr Bishop is your legal guardian, and I have no intention of interfering in any way.'

Her look of relief was unmistakable. 'I thank you for your understanding. I know that my uncle and your father were not good friends; that until we appeared, your family would have stood to inherit his fortune. I hope that this change of circumstances will not be a problem for you.'

No sooner had she spoken than Sapphire realised she had offended him. His eyes flashed and his lips thinned, and her heart thudded uncomfortably. He viewed her down his aristocratic nose and an unwelcome heat suffused her cheeks. She would not remain at his side to be given a set-down, however well-deserved. She dug her heel in and clicked her tongue and Starlight responded immediately. They cantered off before he could say what he was thinking about her impertinence. She must learn to curb her tongue. She had no wish to anger him, for he might rescind his previous remark and start taking an active interest in her life as was his legal right.

His huge stallion was quite capable of overtaking her, but for some reason he did not do so, instead allowing her to return alone. She was unused to dealing with prickly, toplofty aristocrats; was more at home talking to less elevated gentlemen. She sincerely regretted inviting him to join them for the picnic, as he was bound to say something to upset her and her family.

When she clattered into the stable yard, Billy was waiting to take the mare. 'Lord Ilchester will be here in a moment; you must make sure his stallion is fed and watered so he is well-rested before he has to return.'

Billy tugged his forelock and grinned. 'He's right behind you, miss, and don't look none too pleased about it neither.'

This was sufficient impetus to cause Sapphire to fling herself from the saddle and scamper off into the house. A clock struck one; this whole debacle had taken place in less than an hour. She was tempted to remain hiding in her room until the autocratic stranger departed, but this would ruin her brothers' name day and she had no intention of being so selfish.

Jenny was waiting for her and it was a matter of moments to step into a fresh gown, this one of pale green dimity with matching slippers and a pretty chip straw bonnet. She tied the ribbons of her headgear over her damp hair, satisfied she looked her best.

She paused on the landing to glance through the window, hoping to see Lord Ilchester sitting at the table, but only her uncle and her brothers were there. Two footmen and a parlourmaid were on their way with trays piled high with delicious food. Calling this meal a picnic was really a misnomer; it was just a meal served in the fresh air.

An impulse made Sapphire take a secondary flight of stairs and exit through the garden room. She had no wish to be confronted by their unwanted guest, as she had no doubt he would have something extremely unpleasant to say to her. If he was indeed lurking in the vestibule in the hope of catching her, he would be disappointed.

Her brothers saw her approaching and waved and called out in excitement. 'We have been waiting ages, and we are as hungry as a horse, aren't we David?'

She stooped to kiss both of them on the top of their fair curls, then took an empty seat beside her uncle. She noticed there was an extra place set and glanced towards the house. Sure enough, his lordship was striding towards them; but instead of looking fierce, he was smiling. He really was a handsome man when he smiled. If she was to be asked her preference, it would be for a man with fair hair and the romantic look of a poet. However, this gentleman was broad-shouldered, stood at least two yards high and had dark brown hair. That his eyes were cerulean blue, and not brown or hazel, made his appearance even more remarkable.

Her uncle pushed himself upright and walked across to greet their guest, but they spoke too softly for her to overhear. They both seemed satisfied with the exchange and came to join the others for the party luncheon.

The boys behaved impeccably, while Uncle John and his lordship seemed to be the best of friends, the conversation ebbing and flowing around the table as if they had been acquainted for years and not just met this day. When they were replete she expected Ilchester to depart, but instead he suggested they play a game of rounders.

'I believe we have the necessary equipment in the boathouse, my lord, but I have not the slightest notion exactly where,' said John. 'Boys, why don't you take our guest and see if you can find what we need?' He beckoned to Jarvis, who had been sitting in the shade with his back to the boathouse. 'Young man, see if you can round up some more lads to play this game; there must be stableboys and garden boys who can be spared from their duties for an hour or so.'

The boys skipped around his lordship in their eagerness to find the items necessary to play the game, and Sapphire watched them vanish into the boathouse. 'As long as I do not have to play, I shall be content. Uncle John, I am not sure this is a good idea. My brothers have never played the game and they are far too small to face a hard ball bowled by an adult.'

'I am sure that Ilchester will devise a game that is suited to their age. You must join in, my dear. It would seem churlish not to.'

'It would seem foolish to do so, in my opinion. I am severely disadvantaged by my gown; I cannot run and neither can I bat. I know that some intrepid young ladies play cricket, but I am not one of those, and I shall sit out and watch.'

He accepted her decision with good grace. 'I shall be the umpire. Good, half a dozen extra players are arriving. I think we should have some sort of competitive games at your party, Sapphire. You do not need to participate yourself, but I'm quite sure others will wish to do so. A tug of war is always popular.'

He wandered off to greet the youngsters and explain what was required of them. By the time he had done so, Ilchester had emerged carrying an armful of wooden posts, while Thomas and David had a bat each and were almost beside themselves with excitement.

With so many willing hands, posts were soon placed correctly and a marker put where the bowler and the batsmen must stand. To Sapphire's astonishment, the gentleman she had thought arrogant and supercilious discarded his jacket and neckcloth and rolled up his shirtsleeves. He looked across at her sitting grimly at the table, and instead of coming over he roared across the grass at her. 'We insist that you join in, Miss Stanton. David and Thomas will be devastated if you do not. How can you refuse them on their anniversary?'

Although she was an excellent horsewoman and prepared to turn her hand to any sort of physical activity, she was hopeless at anything that required co-ordination. She was as likely to hit the ball as she was to fly to the moon. But he was quite right to chide her. She must put aside her imminent humiliation for the sake of her brothers' enjoyment.

Reluctantly, she stood up and went to join the eager throng of players. She had a horrible feeling this was not going to end well for her.

5

The miscellany of participants joined in the game with gusto. Even though neither of the boys managed to catch or hit the ball, they had great fun running from base to base. Sapphire's attempts at scoring a rounder were pathetic, and the first time she ran she put her slipper through the skirt of her dress and fell flat on her face.

His lordship had her back on her feet as if she weighed no more than a bag of feathers. 'I can see why you had no wish to play, Miss Stanton. You have ruined your gown and it is entirely my fault.' He looked so contrite that she forgave him at once for his insistence that she join in.

'For all your faults, sir — and I'm sure they are legion — I cannot hold you responsible for tearing my gown.' Her brothers, who ran in tandem, were running round a post, oblivious to her problems. 'If you will excuse me, my lord, I shall return to the house and see what can be done to repair the damage.' As Meg and Jenny, their skirts hitched up in a most unflattering way, had opted to play, she could depart knowing her brothers were well supervised. Uncle John had abandoned his position as umpire and was snoozing comfortably in his bath chair.

'I have no wish to shout across the grass to my brothers, so would you be kind enough to tell them why I have gone inside?'

Gideon grinned, making him look less austere and far more approachable. 'It will be my absolute pleasure, Miss Stanton. I give you my word the boys will come to no harm in your absence.'

As he was presently the bowler, the game could not proceed until he returned to his position. Billy was waiting patiently to receive the ball, and Sapphire hurriedly removed herself from the field of play. On her return to the house she examined the tear in her gown, and was relieved to see that a few stitches would be sufficient to repair it.

She had discarded her bonnet long ago, and the late afternoon sun warmed her back as she returned. She decided to visit the stables and check Lord Ilchester's mount was ready for the long ride back.

Ned appeared from a loose box, his face concerned. 'His lordship's horse is lame, miss. He won't be able to ride him for a day or two. I don't reckon either of the horses we have will be up to his weight.'

'Then he will have to remain here until Sultan is recovered. I expect somebody from Ilchester Abbey will arrive tomorrow to discover what has delayed him, so there is no need for anyone to take a message today.'

Once inside she summoned the housekeeper and butler. She explained the problem to them. 'Robinson, do you have a footman who could act as a valet for Lord Ilchester?'

'I do, Miss Stanton. I shall send him to speak to the master's man immediately. His lordship will require toiletries and a nightshirt, which can be borrowed from Mr Bishop.'

'Mrs Banks, you must inform Cook that we will require a formal dinner to be served this evening. The boys will be exhausted after running about all day and they will require nothing else to eat. We shall use the small dining room; it would be ridiculous for the three of us to be marooned around the huge table in the grand dining room.'

'I shall have a room prepared for him, miss. Shall I send you a maid to stitch your gown?'

'Thank you. I must return and inform Lord Ilchester that his stallion's lame as soon as possible.'

It took longer than she had hoped to restore her appearance, but fortunately the noisy ball game was still in full swing. Although it would not be dark for several hours already, the shadows were lengthening and the nightingales had begun to sing.

As Sapphire approached, the game ended amidst general applause. Jenny hurried towards her, her face wreathed in smiles and running with perspiration. 'My word, that was a grand afternoon, and no mistake. We never thought to play rounders with a lord.'

'I'm glad everyone enjoyed themselves,' said Sapphire. 'Lord Ilchester's horse is lame and he will be unable to return tonight. Fortunately, as he has no luggage with him, I shall not have to wear an evening gown. However, I wish to bathe and put something more formal on. The boys must go to bed without joining us downstairs. Please make sure that Meg is aware of this.'

The matter of her brothers successfully arranged, she now had to speak to her uncle and his lordship. The stableboys and garden lads had dispersed and her brothers, with the help of their guest, were collecting up the paraphernalia associated with their game. This gave her the opportunity to speak to her uncle before she was obliged to inform his lordship that, whether he liked it or not, he would have to stay the night at Canfield Hall.

'I rather think he was angling for an invitation, my dear. I don't think he has enjoyed himself so much for years.'

'Are you feeling well enough to remain up for dinner, Uncle John?'

'I had a splendid nap whilst they were playing. I am feeling better than I have for years.'

Jarvis appeared and trundled her aged relative away. Meg and Jenny emerged from the boathouse, each holding a grubby boy by the hand. Much to her consternation, Sapphire found herself quite alone, and for a moment was quite nervous.

Ilchester strolled across, nonchalantly rolling his sleeves down his tanned and muscular arms. He flicked his coat from the back of a chair and shrugged it on. Sapphire had never seen a gentleman do this and it made her feel rather peculiar. Indeed, the whole afternoon had been strange and unlike anything she had experienced before.

When she explained about his stallion, he shrugged. 'It seems that I must apologise yet again, Miss Stanton. I had no intention of foisting myself on you overnight, but I must own that I am not at all sorry I do not have to ride back this evening. I am quite exhausted after so much unaccustomed activity.' He said this with a straight face but she knew he was jesting.

'I had thought that maybe you would like to send a message to Ilchester, but on reflection I don't believe anyone who works here would be able to find their way before dark.'

'There is no need to worry, Miss Stanton. I doubt that my mother or sisters will even notice my absence. They are attending a soirée this evening and will be taken up with that.'

'I cannot imagine any social event that could possibly take precedence over the well-being of my family.' When he raised an eyebrow she giggled.

'Actually, as I have never attended a social event of any sort I have no idea whether I would feel the same as Lady Ilchester and your sisters about the matter.'

'Not even made morning calls?'

She shook her head, beginning to enjoy this light-hearted badinage. 'Although my mama was from a wealthy family, she was disowned when she eloped with my papa. When he died we lived in straitened circumstances until Mr Palmer arrived and took care of us. He was not a rich man either, but we managed very well.' She gazed around the many acres of parkland and back to the palatial house in which she now resided. 'We are fortunate indeed to have found a haven here with Mr Bishop. Although we have been here several weeks, I am still not quite accustomed to being able to have whatever I want no matter what the cost.'

Gideon had collected his mangled neckcloth and held it up with a rueful smile. 'I fear this is past redemption,

Miss Stanton. I hope that I might find a fresh one before we dine tonight.' He offered his arm and without hesitation she placed her hand on it, and together they ambled towards the house.

The silence was companionable, not oppressive in any way. Gideon was a surprisingly easy gentleman to spend time with. Before she could prevent herself, Sapphire had issued him and his family with an invitation to attend her birthday celebrations next month. To her astonishment, his eyes blazed and the muscles beneath her hand tensed.

'We should be delighted to come. There is nothing the ladies of my family like better than attending a house party. Will you have a ball in the evening, after the garden party?'

'I had not thought of doing so, but if there are sufficient couples there is no reason why we should not dance after dinner. I shall be engaging musicians to entertain during the afternoon, so they might as well remain for the evening.'

'No doubt Mr Bishop has a list of all the notable families in the area, but I should be happy to supply you with the names of my friends and neighbours who live within driving distance of this estate.'

'Thank you, that is most kind of you. My uncle is determined that I shall become a social butterfly. I am not comfortable at the thought of mixing with dozens of strangers; I much prefer to spend my time with my family.'

They had now reached the elegant marble staircase that led to the terrace which ran along the front of the house. Abruptly Sapphire removed her hand and skipped up ahead of him. She glanced over her shoulder. 'I shall see you at dinner, my lord. I must oversee my brothers as they get ready to retire.' Being in such close proximity to him was making her feel quite dizzy.

Her brothers were already in their nightshirts and tucking into coddled eggs and slices of succulent pink ham when she arrived in the nursery. They had moved to the upper floor when Meg had been appointed as the nursemaid, and were perfectly happy having their own domain.

'Have you enjoyed yourselves today, boys?' Sapphire asked them.

Tom answered first. 'We did, we did, Saffy. Lord Ilchester said he will give us our first riding lesson tomorrow if we go to bed with no argument.'

She had wondered why everything was so peaceful here. 'That was kind of him. He is a cousin of ours. We share the same great-grandfather — that is to say, our great-grandfather was his grandfather.'

'We didn't know we had a lord in the family. Will we be lords like him one day?' David said as he finished his mouthful.

'No, I'm afraid not, sweetheart. Titles are passed down to a close member of the family, and although he has no sons of his own as yet, he has a younger brother. Also, in your case you are related to him through our mama, so would not be eligible anyway.' This was a strange conversation to be having with a pair of five-year-olds. 'Goodnight, boys. I must go and bathe and change, as I can still smell lake water on my person.'

In her own apartment her maid was waiting for her and had already set out the hip bath behind the screen in her dressing room. There had been no necessity to light the fire, as the room was south-facing and still warm from the sun.

Whilst Sapphire relaxed in the rose-scented water, Jenny untangled her hair so it could be washed. Hopefully it would dry before she was obliged to put it up and dress for dinner, which was to be served at six o'clock tonight to allow Uncle John to rest after the activities of the day.

Although her hair was still a trifle damp, Sapphire decided she could wait no longer to put it up, as it was already a quarter to six. 'I had forgotten I had this gown, Jenny. I ordered so many when we first arrived here.'

'It's an unusual shade, miss, and no mistake. I reckon it's the colour of a duck egg, and very pretty it is too. Not too grand, but smart enough to make a good impression.'

'I think the neckline rather low, but that is probably because I have never worn anything so formal before.' She stood and viewed herself in the mirror. Who was this beautiful stranger who stared back at her? What a difference a lovely gown made to one's appearance.

'There is no need to wait up for me, Jenny; I can see myself to bed. Please leave out my habit, as I shall be riding first thing tomorrow.'

She had no idea where their guest had been put for the night and had not thought to ask. She hesitated in the wide gallery and then crept forward to peer over the balustrade. There was no sound of voices coming from the drawing room, so perhaps Lord Ilchester was not down yet.

Suddenly he was beside her and her

knees all but gave way. 'What are we looking at, Miss Stanton?' he asked smoothly, leaning over the ornate railing.

'I was looking for you, my lord, but obviously in quite the wrong place.' She glared at him. 'If there is one thing that I cannot abide, it is a gentleman who sneaks up on one.'

His eyes were laughing at her and his mouth was twitching. He bowed in a ridiculously overblown way. 'I most humbly beg your pardon, Miss Stanton, for arriving unannounced.'

Her irritation vanished beneath the warmth of his smile. 'You are a most annoying gentleman. I cannot think why my brothers are so taken with you.' For a moment she thought he was going to stretch out and touch her face, and a flash of anticipation held her rigid; then the moment passed.

'I believe we are tardy, Miss Stanton. Your uncle will be wondering what has become of us. And by the way, might I say how lovely you look in that exquisite ensemble.'

This time she did stumble, and only his lightning-fast reflexes prevented her from taking a nasty tumble down the stairs. He did not immediately release her hand, and the warmth of his fingers was doing peculiar things to her pulse. When he released his hold she hastily placed her hand behind her back.

They continued their progress down the stairs. Having him so close caused her to almost lose her footing for a second time, but she was able to steady herself without assistance.

'Forgive me for saying so,' he said conversationally, 'but I believe that you must be the clumsiest young lady of my acquaintance. I'm surprised you have not done yourself serious harm before now.' The outrageous statement steadied her nerves and she was able to stop in order to fix him with her most icy stare.

'And you, sir, are without doubt the most unpleasant and irritating gentleman I have ever met.'

His bark of laughter followed her down the stairs, adding to her annoyance. She shot past the waiting footmen and into the drawing room, leaving him to follow in her wake. Her uncle was nowhere to be seen, but the French doors were open onto the terrace and she could hear the clink of glass out there.

The perfect hostess would wait for her guest and allow him to accompany her, but she would not walk another step with that man beside her. She was known for her good humour, patience and sunny temperament, but in the space of an afternoon all these had deserted her.

'There you are at last, my dear,' said John. 'I have ordered champagne to be served. It is a day of celebration, after all.'

'I have never tasted it, Uncle John, and should be delighted to do so now. I do believe you have caught the sun today. In fact, we are both quite tanned.' She held out her arm for his inspection. She was not wearing gloves — another mark in her disfavour. 'I believe it is considered unladylike to expose oneself to the sunshine, but I am not interested in the silly rules of society. I shall do as I please.'

'Shall you indeed, Miss Stanton? That should make for an interesting party next month,' Lord Ilchester's smooth, annoying voice said from behind her. He was as soft-footed as a cat and appeared to enjoy making her uncomfortable. She ignored his comment; it was of no merit.

'Uncle John, I see we are to dine out here. What an excellent idea.'

One of the new footmen, smartly dressed in livery and wig, held out a silver tray upon which were three glasses of sparkling champagne. Sapphire reached out and took one. 'This is delicious, and quite perfect for a summer evening.'

The table had been set out and laid as if it was in the dining room, with the best silver, fine damask cloth and crystalware. It might be better if she sat; she was bound to trip over something if she remained on her feet. She had an unpleasant fluttering in her stomach and her appetite had deserted her. She was dreading being served a series of delicious dishes and being unable to eat them. The meal was served à la française; the platters were placed centrally and then they were left to help themselves.

After a few minutes, Sapphire realised their guest was paying her no further attention but was instead deeply involved in a discussion of the merits of some political act or other, leaving her to recover her composure and her appetite. There were three courses, each with several removes, and she enjoyed a little of everything.

'I am unable to consume another morsel. I had no idea your cook could produce such excellent food, Uncle John. I shall leave you gentlemen to your port and take a promenade around the garden.'

Both of the men got to their feet and she smiled politely before setting off across the terrace, praying she did not tread on the hem of her gown. The sun was sliding below the horizon, turning the water of the lake a spectacular shade of gold — a perfect ending to a very enjoyable evening.

She strolled around for some time before arriving in the rose garden, where she found her favourite arbour, a stone seat surrounded by sweet-smelling honeysuckle and climbing roses. She had picked up a pebble in her slipper and needed to sit down in order to remove it. She viewed the bench with disfavour — she had no wish to spoil her new gown.

A slight sound alerted her this time, and she was ready when his lordship spoke quietly from behind her. 'Allow me, Miss Stanton.' He removed his handkerchief and spread it on the stone, and she had no alternative but to be seated. Her heart was drumming and her bodice became unaccountably tight. What was it about this gentleman that so disturbed her senses?

6

Sapphire could hardly refuse to sit down now Lord Ilchester had placed his handkerchief on the stone bench. Once she was seated, he folded his long length beside her, thankfully keeping a respectful distance.

'You are proving elusive tonight, Miss Stanton. I have been wandering like a lost sheep around the gardens searching for you this past quarter of an hour.'

'I came out because I wished to be on my own.' The words were somewhat abrupt, but she was too agitated to say more.

Instead of springing to his feet and vanishing into the darkness, his teeth flashed white and he settled himself more comfortably. 'I'm damned if I'm going to apologise for joining you. I seem to have done nothing but grovel since we met this morning.'

His unexpected turn of phrase so shocked her that she forgot she was nervous. 'Kindly moderate your language when talking to me, sir. I do not appreciate hearing such things.'

'I should hardly think you do, sweetheart, but I fear you are going to have to become accustomed to my robust turn of phrase.'

His reply almost gave her palpitations. He had no right to use such endearments, nor to refuse to beg her pardon for swearing. She had come to the rose garden to find peace and quiet but had found quite the reverse.

'Lord Ilchester, you forget yourself. We are barely acquainted — '

'How true that is. But you forget that I am, I believe, your true guardian, and can therefore talk to you as I would one of my sisters.'

This was the outside of enough. What he said might be a fact of law, but as far as she was concerned Uncle John held that position, and she had no intention of allowing this intruder to interfere with her life in any way.

'You did not know of my existence until this morning, so you can hardly claim to be an interested party.' She jumped to her feet and scowled down at him lounging, unabashed and amused, in the arbour. 'I sincerely hope that someone sends a carriage to collect you tomorrow, Ilchester, because you are no longer welcome at Canfield Hall.'

In one smooth movement he was on his feet — no longer relaxed and friendly, but rigid with disapproval. Referring to him without his title was disrespectful, and her actual comment was hardly polite, so it was not surprising he was angry.

She knew instinctively he would not harm her, and it was easier to deal with him when he was glaring at her than when he was being charming and friendly. In fact, she was rather enjoying the exchange. Having him towering over her was a trifle intimidating, but she was better able to cope with his anger than his charm.

'I know why your father sent his man here every year,' she said. 'It was not to offer assistance to my uncle, but to see if he was still alive. As you are no longer a beneficiary, I assume that your interest in Canfield Hall has come to an end.'

She was sure she actually heard his teeth grind. What had possessed her to say something so inflammatory and impertinent? In the near darkness she could not see his face clearly, but the ominous silence told her all she needed to know. Deciding that discretion was the better part of valour, she gathered her skirts and prepared to run away.

'Remain where you are, Miss Stanton.' His voice cracked like a whip and she almost obeyed him, but something told her it would be wiser to remove herself immediately from his vicinity. He was a formidable gentleman and she had no wish to be given a bear-garden jaw, even if it was justified.

She scampered through the gardens,

expecting at any minute to be accosted by this furious giant of a man. He must have become lost, as she arrived safely at the terrace. The drawing room doors were open, and the evidence of their dinner had been removed.

She was relieved to be back safely, but remained outside for a few minutes until her heart had stopped hammering and she was less breathless. She had no wish to alarm her uncle by appearing red-faced and distressed, as he might think his lordship had taken liberties, though the exact opposite was true.

Now the excitement of the confrontation had dissipated, Sapphire was ashamed of her behaviour, and instead of creeping away to her apartment she decided to wait and apologise to their guest. Why was he taking so long? He had longer legs than she, and the candles flickering in the windows of the house were quite visible from the rose garden.

'Why are you dithering about out here, Miss Stanton? Surely you are not afraid to meet me after your disgraceful behaviour?'

The apology she had been rehearsing in her head evaporated like snow in the sunshine. She spun and stared up at Gideon with dislike. 'I thought you had become lost or had had an accident, and I was about to go in search of you. I should have realised you were creeping about, as usual, and waiting to upset me.'

He stepped onto the terrace and for some reason her feet remained glued to the paving stones. He closed the gap between them until he was no more than an arm's length away. 'Mr Bishop has retired, and I took the liberty of dismissing your staff.'

Sapphire swallowed nervously. He could not have made it more clear — he had sent everyone away so he was free to administer whatever retribution he thought fit without fear of witnesses or interruption.

'In which case, sir, you are now free to give me the dressing-down I so richly deserve. I have behaved appallingly. I am not normally outspoken or impertinent, and I sincerely apologise for — '

'I will hear no more of that, Miss Stanton. I have no wish to admonish you or to hear you apologise.' He raised both hands in a gesture of supplication. 'Please, can we start again? We have been at loggerheads most of the day and that is the last thing I want.' He was quite irresistible when he wasn't scowling at her.

'We have both behaved badly, although I sincerely believe that I am more culpable than you.'

He was waiting — not exactly smiling, but his eyes had a definite twinkle. Her reservations about him vanished and she returned his smile. 'Yes, please let us begin again,' she said. 'I shall go into the drawing room and from that moment we are strangers.' Not waiting for him to comment, she almost skipped through the French doors, and was obliged to take several steadying breaths before she was ready to step out onto the terrace again. She was beginning to enjoy this play-acting — it had been far too long since she had been able to have fun on her own account.

He was half-sitting on the stone balustrade and immediately jumped to his feet upon her reappearance. He bowed deeply and she curtsied. They were at an impasse; if this was to be done correctly there should be a person to introduce them. Then he strolled towards her.

'Good evening. I believe I have the pleasure of speaking to Miss Stanton. Allow me to introduce myself. I am Gideon Frederick William Bishop, Lord Ilchester. I am your cousin.'

She curtsied again. 'I am delighted to make your acquaintance, my lord. I am Miss Sapphire Stanton; and Mr Bishop, with whom I am residing at present, is my great-uncle.'

He grinned, his teeth white in the darkness. 'Do you care to promenade, Miss Stanton? There is much I must tell you about my family, for you and your brothers are part of it now.'

As they strolled a discreet distance apart, he told her about his sisters, mother and brother, and she returned the favour. She was puzzled that he did not appear to be overly fond of his siblings, as he had so obviously enjoyed being with her brothers.

'I must go in, my lord. I heard the village clock striking midnight a moment ago. I believe that you have promised to teach my brothers to ride, and you can be very sure they will be up and waiting in the stable yard at first light.'

He chuckled; a rich dark sound. 'In which case, we had better say good-night. I have had the most enjoyable day. I cannot remember when I have had so much fun before. I shall see you in the stable yard first thing tomorrow morning.'

He half-bowed and she dipped in a small curtsy. He had the courtesy to allow her to go in alone and not prowl along behind her as he had done previously. When she reached the safety of the gallery she risked a glance back, and to her astonishment she saw he was extinguishing the candles — doing a servant's job without a second thought. As he had dismissed the staff, she supposed it was his responsibility to make sure the house was safe before he retired. However, he was a guest, and if anyone should be doing this it was she. Too late to repine; she would thank him tomorrow.

★ ★ ★

Gideon watched Sapphire almost run away from him and wished they hadn't got off to such a poor start. Mind you, they had spent a pleasant hour conversing before she dashed away.

He had told her categorically that he was now her legal guardian, but he wasn't entirely sure this was the case. In fact, the more he thought about it, the less likely it seemed that he

110

had inherited three wards along with his father's estates and gambling debts. He paused as he was extinguishing the final candelabra. He recalled an incident much talked about in town a year or so ago, when Sir Giles something-or-other died intestate and a reprobate uncle stepped in to claim the position as guardian and control of the considerable fortunes of the orphaned children. He seemed to remember that the young lady and gentleman in question were below their majority, but no longer children, and they had applied to the Courts of Chancery to appoint their own guardian; this was upheld. One thing he knew for certain was that society and the law did not approve of any romantic liaison between a guardian and his ward.

Startled by this thought, he knocked over his own candlestick, leaving him in inky blackness. He cursed under his breath. No point in grovelling for the object, as he had no idea where the tinderbox was stored and, being mid-summer, there were no fires alight for him to use. He would have to make his way upstairs by touch alone.

As he groped his way to the doors that led into the spacious hall, he reviewed what had made him drop his candle. He had known Sapphire Stanton for less than a day. Was it possible he was already thinking of her romantically?

By the time he had crossed the hall, his eyes had become accustomed to the lack of light and he could now see sufficiently well to continue his journey to his bedchamber without fear of breaking his neck. The more he considered this extraordinary notion, the more he liked it. Although he was not actually hanging out for a wife, there was something about this woman that excited him. That she was beautiful was beyond doubt, but she was also intelligent, kind and strong-willed — an irresistible combination as far as he was concerned.

He reached his room having only barked his shins once and stopped a couple of times. He did not bother to light a lamp, as he was going to retire immediately. The footman who had been appointed as his valet had long gone to his bed, but Gideon was quite capable of disrobing without assistance. There was a nightshirt folded neatly on the end of the bed, but he tossed this to one side. He preferred to sleep as nature intended.

★   ★   ★

Sapphire was up and dressed before her brothers woke and was able to oversee their dressing. Particular care was needed this morning if they were to sit astride their ponies.

'We don't want to have breakfast now, Saffy. We want to have it after our ride,' David said.

'We can go out to the stables now, but I don't promise Lord Ilchester will be there. It is extremely early, but I am sure that between us Ned, Billy and I can manage.'

No sooner were they out of the house when the boys shot ahead, eager to be the first to arrive in the yard. Sapphire took a more leisurely pace, as running in the voluminous skirt of her habit would be hazardous.

There was no need for her to hurry. His lordship must have been there before them, despite the fact it had not yet struck eight o'clock. Her mare was waiting but there was no sign of her brothers, their ponies or Lord Ilchester.

'Ned, where have they all gone?'

'His lordship reckons they would do best to be led about the place; get the feeling of being in the saddle. He and Billy are gone for a walk around the park.'

'In which case I shall join them later, but first I shall ride through the woods. There is no need for you to accompany me, Ned. I shall not be going out of the grounds this morning.'

He tossed her aboard. She rammed

her foot into the single-stirrup iron, gathered up the reins and was ready to leave. The sun was already hot on her back. No doubt the boys would wish to continue their swimming lessons later on. The thought of being in the lake appealed to her, but under no circumstances would she do so whilst their guest was still in residence.

'How is the stallion? Is he sound enough to ride today?'

'Not a chance, miss. He's pulled a tendon and will have to stay here for at least a week. His lordship sent one of the new men with a message this morning; right early it was. He will be sending for his baggage. He don't seem in no hurry to leave, that's for sure.'

She wasn't sure if this was good news or bad, but was definitely relieved their guest had not been in the yard to hear Ned speaking about him so freely. She set off in the opposite direction to the park, taking the tradesman's route that led directly into the acres of woodland that surrounded the rear of the property.

Once in the shelter of the trees she relaxed. Her heavy wool habit was far too hot for this weather. She must arrange for the local seamstress to make her something more suitable for the summer, perhaps in moss green with gold buttons.

The mare ambled along and Sapphire's thoughts returned to Ned's words. Canfield Hall was vast; accommodating a single house guest would make no difference at all. However, she was not comfortable at the notion of spending the next week in the company of this very attractive gentleman. They would be obliged to dine together. Even if they stayed apart during the day, it would inevitably lead to spending several hours alone in his company after her uncle retired. This would not be a good idea, in her opinion. For some reason she behaved like a shrew when he was close and said things she immediately regretted.

The mare shied as a pheasant flew

out under her feet and Sapphire almost lost her seat. Once she was sorted and settled again, she decided she would increase their pace. The sun-dappled path stretched invitingly ahead of her, quite long enough to gallop if she so wished.

She clicked her tongue and transferred her weight to the front of the saddle and immediately the horse responded. The wind whipped through her hair, dislodging her hat and sending it flying into the branches. There was an inviting five-barred gate a hundred yards ahead and she decided to take the mare over it.

As the mare gathered herself to jump, Sapphire realised she had no clear idea of what was on the other side of the obstacle. She sent up a fervent prayer to the Almighty that she had not made a catastrophic mistake.

7

Gideon was enjoying the early-morning walk with the twins. He had been away at school and university when his siblings were this age and he sincerely wished he had not missed this delightful stage of their development. He was leading Tom on his pony and Billy had David beside him. They walked sedately down the track that led towards the woods.

'Billy, where does that path lead to?' he asked. 'It should be cooler in the shade of the hedge.'

'I've not been down it, my lord, but I reckon it runs around the wood and will bring us out behind the house.' The path was on the right-hand side of the trees and on the left of the open parkland.

'Then we shall take it. Are you enjoying your first experience of riding?' Gideon asked the boys. 'You both seem to have a good seat.'

'Can we go a bit faster, sir?' Tom asked. 'We won't fall off, will we, David?'

'Hold on to the neck strap if you feel insecure. Whatever you do, don't snatch at the reins. Are you ready? Relax into the saddle and go with the motion of the pony.' He patted the animal's neck and began to walk faster. As soon as he was sure both boys were happy with the increasing pace, he started to run.

The ponies trotted smartly and Tom and David screeched with excitement, but both remained clinging limpet-like to the saddle. They were approaching a break in the trees. It was possible that there was fresh path ahead that led into the woods. This might shorten the distance back to the stables. They had been out for half an hour, and an hour was quite long enough for a first lesson.

'David, Tom, pull gently on your reins, for we are going to turn into the woods in a moment.' Perspiration was trickling unpleasantly down his face, and he wished he'd had the sense to leave off his stock and jacket before racing about in the sunshine.

The pony he was leading obediently dropped from a trot to a walk. He was about to dip into his pocket and remove his handkerchief when the unmistakable sound of a galloping horse made him pause. He flung himself against the pony and pushed it violently into the hedge not a moment too soon.

★   ★   ★

Sapphire peered through the mare's pricked ears as they soared into the air and was relieved to see an open expanse of parkland the other side of the gate. Thank goodness! Then, to her horror, from the corner of her eye she saw there was someone directly in her path.

It was too late to take avoiding action. There was nothing she could do but pray that whoever it was would fling themselves out of the way. Unfortunately Starlight also saw the movement to her left and pecked on landing. Then Sapphire was sailing through the air; she landed on her back with such a thud the breath was knocked from her lungs.

As she lay gasping she gradually became aware that someone was beside her. She was gaping like a fish out of water, her head was spinning, and for a second she didn't recognise the gentleman on his knees. Then her vision cleared. Lord Ilchester was preventing her from sitting up.

Slowly she recovered her breath and was able to speak. 'The boys — are they unhurt?' She struggled, but the pressure on her shoulders remained firm.

He nodded. 'They are both perfectly well. Don't move for a moment; you could have injured your spine. That was a hard fall you took.'

She relaxed and reassured him, 'I can move all my limbs, and apart from being winded I am certain I have suffered no injury.'

He watched while she wriggled her toes and waved her fingers in the air and then sat back. 'You may get up now, Miss Stanton.' He did not offer to assist but turned his back and strode across to where her brothers were sitting quietly on their ponies. Billy was holding the leading reins of both animals.

Puzzled by his abrupt departure, Sapphire spent several minutes attempting to breathe normally and then to scramble to her feet. She winced when she put her weight on her right ankle and was relieved nobody else had been injured by her unexpected arrival. Her mare was grazing a few yards away and was obviously uninjured. She limped across and collected the reins, which were trailing on the ground. 'Well then, my girl, that was our first mishap. I am glad neither of us suffered from my foolishness.'

This detour to collect her mount had taken only a minute or so, but when she looked across she discovered she was alone. Her intention had been to apologise profusely for her stupidity and thank Gideon for the speedy reactions that had kept her brothers safe from harm. Where on earth were they?

She stared down the path in both directions but could not see them. How could they have vanished so speedily? She suppressed her anger at being abandoned; she deserved to be sent to Coventry. After all, she could have caused a serious accident.

Although Starlight was not much more than fifteen hands, she could not remount without assistance. Obviously his lordship's intention was to punish her by making her walk home. She ached from head to toe, and although she had insisted she was uninjured, she had twisted her right ankle quite severely. There was no possibility at all that she could walk the mile or so back to Canfield Hall, so somehow she must get onto the saddle.

Then she remembered she had just jumped the gate. This would be ideal to use as a mounting block. 'Come along, sweetheart. You must stand quietly for me so I can get up.'

Then she understood why she had been unable to see her brothers. The gate stood open: they had taken a different route home. With some difficulty she scrambled up the bars and manoeuvred herself until she was secure. Once she was safely settled, she clicked her tongue and the mare moved smoothly forward.

Even with no weight on her injury, every movement made by the horse sent waves of pain so severe she was forced to bite her lip to avoid fainting. At this painfully slow pace she would take an age to reach the stables. By the time she arrived she was no longer apologetic, but incandescent with rage. The pain from her ankle was making her feel quite nauseous, but she would not cast up her accounts until she had spoken her mind to Ilchester.

Once Gideon had made sure Sapphire was unharmed, his rage at her stupidity made him want to shake some sense into her. When he had seen her crash to the ground his world had tilted on its axis. For a terrifying second he had believed her dead, and he had ceased to breathe. This relief was rapidly replaced by ire, and he knew that if he remained within arm's reach of her he would do something he would regret.

He did not believe in corporal punishment, but at this moment he was barely restraining himself from administering a well-deserved spanking to the chit who could have killed herself and her brother. But now was not the time to tell her what he thought of her behaviour; that could keep until he had recovered his temper.

He left her struggling to sit up and strode back to the boys. 'Billy, get the gate open. We are going home that way.' He managed a feeble grin for the two children sitting immobile with shock. 'Your sister is unhurt, lads, but we shall leave her to walk home as punishment for almost killing us.'

Tom giggled nervously. 'Are you sure she is all right? She's making a funny noise.'

'That's what happens when you fall on your back, young man. She will be perfectly well in a moment or two. Now, did you get scratched when we went head first into the hedge?'

'No, and Ned has checked Merry. That was ever so exciting. I never knew riding could be such an adventure.'

Satisfied his charge was not upset, Gideon snatched up the leading rein and followed Billy to the gate, which was already being swung open.

David swivelled in the saddle and called back: 'Saffy won't be able to get on again, sir. Shouldn't Billy help her?'

'She's got to walk back because she's been naughty, David. She shouldn't have jumped over the gate and almost landed on us.' Tom seemed almost gleeful at the thought of his sister having to trudge back on her own.

The ride was declared a great success by the twins and they thanked Gideon prettily. He could hear them telling their nursemaid all about it as she led them away to wash their hands before they had their breakfast.

'Ned, Miss Stanton will not be back for a while. There is no need to send out a search party — Billy will explain why.'

He would return to his chamber and try and spruce himself up before he went to break his fast. He was wearing a borrowed shirt and stock, but was hopeful his own would now be ready for him. After a strip wash he was handed his freshly sponged and pressed breeches, his jacket, his polished Hessians and his own clean shirt.

As he strolled past the nursery stairs he could hear the children laughing and chattering as they ate their breakfast. He had taken his time with his ablutions, and when he checked his pocket watch he discovered the hour had moved on and the time was a little after ten o'clock.

No doubt Miss Stanton would be waiting for him in the breakfast parlour. He had intended to ring a peal over her, but his anger had dissipated and he thought being obliged to walk home was punishment enough for her foolishness. He sincerely hoped she would not bear a grudge.

On entering the parlour he was surprised to find it empty — not even his host was there. A footman was waiting to fetch him his choice of hot beverage and he beckoned him over. 'Has Miss Stanton already eaten?'

'No, my lord, she's not back from her ride yet.'

Devil take it! There was something wrong; she should have been here by now. He turned on his heel and strode through the house and out of the side door that led directly to the stables. There was a commotion coming from the archway and he broke into a run.

Ned greeted Sapphire as she guided the mare onto the cobbles. There was no need to tell him she was in trouble; he had known her since she was an infant in leading strings.

'Here, don't you try and get down, miss. I'll lift you from the saddle.' He yelled for assistance and two stableboys appeared. 'Here, hold onto the mare. She's a mite skittish.'

'I have injured my ankle, Ned. If I had not had the gate to use as a mounting block I would still be abandoned in the other side of the woods.'

Perhaps she would leave the confrontation with Ilchester until she felt better. She was about to place her arm around Ned's neck when his lordship burst into the yard. Without a by your leave he reached out and lifted her from the saddle. A shaft of agony from her ankle made her gasp, and she did not have the energy to protest.

'Sweetheart, this is all my doing. I should have stayed and not stomped off in high dudgeon.' Holding her firmly against his chest, he turned and headed for the house. 'Ned, send someone for the physician. I want him here immediately.'

Somehow she managed to whisper to him, 'Please, take care. Every jolt of my ankle is so painful I believe I might faint from it.'

He said something so rude she hid her flaming cheeks in his jacket. 'I beg your pardon for my language, but I am angry with myself for leaving you the way I did.'

He had slowed his pace, and at a gentle walk she felt more comfortable; well enough to respond. 'I am too unwell to discuss the matter with you at the moment, my lord, but when I am feeling better I shall have much to say to you on the subject, and none of it will be pleasant.'

He did not seem particularly perturbed by this announcement. 'And I do not blame you one jot. I have behaved despicably and deserve anything you throw at me.'

They were now at her bedchamber and he shouldered his way in, shouting for Jenny. Her maid arrived in a flurry of petticoats, her homely face etched with concern.

'Lawks a mussy! Whatever next! Please put Miss Stanton on the daybed, my lord, and I will take care of her now.'

'Very well, I shall leave her in your capable hands.' He placed her carefully on the chaise longue and immediately moved away. From the open door he spoke again. 'I have caused one disaster after another, Miss Stanton, and am well aware that you would wish me to Hades. I give you my word that as soon as I am confident you are not seriously hurt, I shall depart. I apologise yet again for causing you such unnecessary distress.'

Sapphire didn't want him to leave — she wanted to be able to castigate him and then laugh together and be friends. However, she was unable to call him back as Jenny inadvertently touched her ankle and the pain sent her into swooning blackness.

★ ★ ★

Gideon muttered imprecations under his breath as he went in search of Mr Bishop. The old gentleman would not be best pleased that his beloved great-niece had been treated so callously.

The drawing room was empty, so he asked to be taken to his host's private domain. Thank God the young footman did not think it necessary to announce him, but merely knocked on the door and then slipped away unobtrusively as all good servants should.

Jarvis opened the door, his usual smile absent. News of the accident had obviously arrived ahead of him — which was hardly surprising as he'd taken so long getting changed.

'Would it be possible for me to speak to Mr Bishop?' asked Gideon.

'He is not well this morning, my lord. I don't reckon he'll be receiving visitors.' That explained the man's glum features.

'I must have a word with him; it is urgent. Kindly go and ask him if he is able to see me. I take it you have sent for his physician?'

'No, my lord, he won't let me. I don't like the look of him at all — he must have overdone it yesterday. His valet is taking care of him.'

Gideon marched straight in. He intended to convince Bishop to see the doctor when he arrived to attend to Miss Stanton. No — in future he would think of her as Sapphire: a strange and inappropriate name for a beautiful young lady with startling sea-green eyes and chestnut hair. Some maggot had got into her parents at her birth, no doubt, and this accounted for the folly.

Jarvis stomped in from what was

133

presumably the bedchamber. 'He reckons as he will see you, my lord. Will you
come this way?'

Mr Bishop was looking remarkably
perky; his colour was good and his
expression animated. A wave of relief
washed over Gideon — he had become
inordinately fond of the elderly gentleman in the short time he had known
him.

'Come in, come in, my dear fellow.
Jarvis is making too much fuss. I am a
trifle fatigued after all the excitement
yesterday, but not at all unwell, as you
can see for yourself. So, my lord, why
the long features?'

Gideon told him the whole sorry tale.
'I have sent for the doctor. I hope you
will let him examine you before he
departs.'

'I shall have no peace until I agree
— what with you, my valet Fullerton,
and Jarvis making such a fuss about
nothing. I am sure that Sapphire has
suffered no serious harm from her fall.
She will need to rest and keep the foot

elevated for a few days, but she will be perfectly well after that. Now, do sit down, my dear fellow; you are making me dizzy prowling around the room as you are. There is something I wish to speak to you about.'

Gideon folded himself onto a convenient upright chair, crossed his legs at the ankles and waited expectantly.

'I told Sapphire that you were her legal guardian, but this is fustian and we both know it. I stand in that role for all three of them. However, I have sent for my lawyer and intend to add a codicil to the effect that, at my demise, you will assume responsibility. I am making you the boys' guardian. My great-niece is quite able to take care of herself and will be a very wealthy young woman.'

'I should be honoured to be officially named, sir; but surely you would wish Miss Stanton to be involved with their upbringing? Unless you are anticipating kicking the bucket in the next couple of years, I'm certain she will be married by then. She and her husband would expect to raise her brothers.'

The old man smiled. 'Exactly so, my dear fellow. My plan is faultless; if she wishes to remain with her siblings she will not contract a marriage. Therefore she will remain here and not leave me on my own.'

This seemed a selfish point of view, and not one Gideon expected from his host. The old gentleman looked remarkably smug. There was something else going on here that he was not privy to.

Gideon got to his feet and bowed politely. 'I believe I see the doctor's gig approaching down the drive. If you would excuse me, sir, I wish to speak to him before he visits your niece.' He strode to the door and then remembered the other reason he had wished to speak to Bishop. 'I would like to borrow your carriage, if I may. I think it best if I depart immediately after what took place today. Miss Stanton holds me in extreme dislike and will be delighted that I have gone.'

'We must do as you see fit, my lord. After all, you are a peer of the realm and must be eager to get away from us commoners.'

This outrageous comment made Gideon laugh out loud. 'Indeed, sir, you have the right of it. I am far too top-lofty to remain here. However, I sincerely hope that my invitation to attend the house party with my family will not be withdrawn.'

'You can be very certain it will not. Please say your farewells to the children; they will be sad to see you go. Thank you for coming to see me in person — I cannot tell you how much it means to me to be back in contact with my relations, however distant they may be. A few weeks ago I considered myself quite alone in the world, but now I have an abundance of family and am determined to remain on God's earth for at least another decade.'

'I'm delighted to hear you say that, Mr Bishop. Thank you for your hospitality. I shall take my leave very soon, but will return with my mother and sisters next month to celebrate Miss Stanton's birthday. By the by, I have left a note of the names and addresses of acquaintances of mine who live within an hour's drive of here. I can guarantee that all of them are acceptable, and several have daughters of a similar age to Miss Stanton.'

He had deliberately omitted from this list any family that had sons who might be considered a suitable match for his delectable cousin.

8

'There, Miss Stanton — I have finished. A very nasty sprain, but fortunately no worse than that. Keep your limb elevated and remain upstairs for at least two days.'

Sapphire smiled her thanks. 'I cannot believe something as insignificant as a sprain could be so painful. I thank you, Doctor Smith, and I shall endeavour to abide by your instructions.'

The doctor departed and she sent word to the nursery that she was ready for visitors. Her brothers had been prevented by Meg, the nursemaid, from immediately charging downstairs when they had heard about her ankle.

They burst in and were about to fling themselves on top of her when she held out both hands. 'No, boys, you have to be careful and quiet. See, the doctor has bandaged up my ankle and I have it resting on a cushion. You cannot climb onto the bed because it will really hurt me.'

'Can we sit on the floor beside you?' David asked.

'Of course you can. There are plenty of cushions and footstools you can bring over if you don't wish to sit on the floor.'

Eventually they were settled to their satisfaction; and after being reassured that she was perfectly well, apart from being stiff, bruised and having a sprained ankle, they told her all about their riding and how much they loved their ponies. She found it rather unsettling that they mentioned Ilchester's name a dozen times during their tale.

'Ned and Billy are going to give us lessons every single day! Lord Ilchester thinks we will be off the leading rein in no time at all,' David said.

'As soon as I am able I shall come down and watch you. When you are proficient enough we can go out together in the mornings. I shall also continue your swimming lessons.'

The rattle of cutlery and crockery heralded the arrival of her eagerly anticipated, but very delayed, breakfast. 'I am sharp-set, boys. I do hope they have brought up enough for all of us. If they haven't, then I fear I shall not feel inclined to share.'

For a second they looked shocked, and then they giggled. 'We had our breakfast ages ago, but I am quite hungry again, aren't you, David?'

Two of the new parlourmaids staggered in with loaded trays — more than enough for half a dozen starving people, let alone the three of them. After they had eaten, Sapphire sent the boys out to play with their puppy.

'Jenny, I wish to speak to Lord Ilchester. Do think you could find him for me?'

Her maid returned with the news that his lordship was speaking to her brothers and would come and see her after that. What seemed like an interminable time later, there was a sharp knock on the door. Sapphire had dismissed Jenny, as what she had to say to this gentleman was best said in private.

As far as she was aware, it was perfectly in order to entertain a member of one's family in one's own sitting room without causing eyebrows to be raised.

'Come in, if you please.' She was relieved that her voice didn't betray her nervousness. Her initial fury had abated, and he *had* apologised most handsomely; but she wished to have matters right between them, especially if he was leaving later today. Also, he had begun to sprinkle his conversation with unnecessary, and inappropriate, endearments and she wished him to stop that at once.

The door slowly opened — somehow she had expected it to be thrown back dramatically. Lord Ilchester stepped in, looking remarkably smart for a man who had arrived with no change of raiment.

'You have changed your jacket, my lord. Am I to take it your valet and baggage have arrived?'

'How observant of you, Miss Stanton. They have indeed. I must admit I looked a trifle shabby. I am famous for my sartorial elegance; a veritable tulip of fashion as you can see.'

His jacket was superbly cut, but a plain dark green; nothing flamboyant at all. His waistcoat was grey silk, and his shirt points and neckcloth nothing out of the ordinary. Then she saw he was having difficulty hiding his amusement at her expense.

For a second she intended to give him a severe set-down for his teasing, but then she laughed instead. 'I do so enjoy the company of a gentleman with a sense of humour.' She waved airily towards an armchair, which was a suitable distance from her daybed. 'In fact, my lord, if you had not abandoned me without ascertaining how I did, I might almost like you.'

He made no move to follow her

gesture. 'I should not have done so, but I was furious with you. Didn't you realise that jumping over a gate without ensuring there was no one passing by was the height of foolhardiness? If I had not pushed Tom and Merry into the hedge they could have been killed.'

A wave of nausea engulfed Sapphire and for a moment she thought she might disgrace herself. She swallowed hastily, took several deep breaths, and the danger passed. 'I had no idea we had come so close to a catastrophe. Small wonder you were angry and decided I should walk home.'

'Promise me you will never do anything so stupid again. I might not be your guardian, but I am head of the family, and believe I have the right to an opinion on this matter.'

'Of course I will not do it again. And on another subject entirely, sir: as you now have your man and your luggage, why don't you stay until your stallion is sound?'

He had been leaning nonchalantly

against the wall, but at her suggestion he appeared to lose his balance. He recovered smoothly and his smile made her feel decidedly peculiar.

'Unfortunately, I have already bid my adieux to your brothers and your uncle, so can hardly remain after that.'

'That is doing it too brown, sir. I am quite certain you do exactly as you please with little regard for anybody's opinion on the matter.' She should not have said that — what had got into her today?

He didn't bother to answer until he was settled opposite, and then he folded his arms and pursed his lips before replying. 'I cannot tell you how happy it makes me, my dear, to know you hold me in such high opinion. For I am thoroughly disliked at home; my staff live in constant fear of being dismissed, and my family of being locked in the attic on a diet of bread and water.'

She put her finger on her lips as if considering his outrageous statement. 'In which case, my lord, the longer you remain here, the better it will be for those at Ilchester Abbey.'

'You are without doubt, miss, an impudent baggage. I believe that it behoves me to stay here until I have shown you the error of your ways.'

His lips twitched, but for a horrible moment she had thought he was serious. 'I think, Lord Ilchester, you would have more success teaching a pig to fly.'

How long this enjoyable badinage could have continued before she said something outrageous was debatable. He laughed at her silliness, and then his expression sobered as if he thought it inappropriate. He was going to leave, and she had something she wished to ask him before he did so.

'My lord, as you are now going to stay until Sultan is fit, could I prevail upon you to do me an enormous favour? Although the estate is in good heart, and the factor and my uncle's man of business are honest hard-working men, I fear Canfield Hall is lagging behind in terms of improvements and innovations. Would you be willing to ride around the estate and see what might be done to improve productivity and the lot of our tenants and workers?'

He nodded. 'I should be delighted, Miss Stanton. However, it would not be civil of me to do so without informing Mr Bishop.' He stood up and strolled to the door, calling back as he exited: 'You must dress for dinner tonight. I have my evening rig here and will be disappointed if I cannot wear it.'

She yelled her reply at his departing back: 'In case you haven't noticed, I am unable to leave this daybed and must not put any weight on my foot for two days.'

He reversed and turned to stare at her through narrowed eyes. 'Shouting is most unladylike, Miss Stanton. I am not an imbecile, and am well aware of your infirmity. I shall, of course, carry you down.'

Before she could protest at his

high-handed suggestion, he vanished and she could hear him whistling merrily as he walked away. The man was too fond of having his own way, and she was not going to allow herself to be carried about the place like an unwanted parcel. There was only one way she could prevent him from carrying out his unacceptable suggestion, and she was determined to put this plan into action and thwart his scheme.

It was difficult to settle with her book after he had gone. Her ankle throbbed unpleasantly, and she needed the commode. She stretched out and rang the little brass bell, relieved when Jenny and a chambermaid came at once.

★   ★   ★

Gideon reached the gallery and for an insane moment was tempted to slide down the polished banister. By rights he should be in a sombre mood. After all, his parent had only been dead just over four months. However, he had never felt so invigorated in his life. There was something inviting about Canfield Hall, and he was more than happy to remain for another few days.

He informed the butler of his change of plans, and the man seemed inordinately pleased. There was something havey-cavey going on and Gideon was determined to discover what it was. His host was having a nap and could not be spoken to, but he was assured a message would be taken as soon as Mr Bishop was awake.

In fact, Gideon had had no intention of departing today, and had been certain Sapphire would ask him to stay on. His luggage was being unpacked at this very moment, and the carriage would already be unharnessed and put away. In his note to his mother he had said he would be staying for a day or two, but had also given her the good news of the invitation to join the Bishops for the house party next month.

Now was as good a time as any to check his stallion's progress. He was halfway to the stable when the fog in his brain cleared and he saw what his elderly relative was about. The intention was for Sapphire to become his wife — that way she would remain with her brothers.

A surge of excitement made him catch his breath. Was this why he felt so happy? Was it possible that he already had warm feelings for his cousin? They had been acquainted barely twenty-four hours — could he have fallen in love so quickly?

His head was spinning. He didn't know if he was confusing desire with a genuine emotion. There was no doubt at all that he found her desirable, and would love to share his bed with her, but was this the same as being in love? All this was new to him. He had never had the slightest interest in any other young lady, even though he had met dozens of hopeful debutantes over the past few years.

He needed to get away from here and clear his head, but it was impossible at the moment. Both the horses that had pulled the barouche would also go under saddle, but they could not be ridden so soon after their long journey. Fortunately, there was nothing up to his weight in the stables.

He would walk around the lake. He was about to head off in that direction when a puppy of indeterminate ancestry shot through the archway, hotly pursued by the twins. Gideon had the foresight to reach down and snatch the wriggling animal from the path before it vanished into the bushes.

'He ran away, sir. He's a very naughty puppy.' Tom held out his arms and Gideon handed him the little dog.

'Silly is ever so sweet, but he doesn't come to his name,' David said.

Gideon dropped to his haunches beside them. 'I'm not surprised if you have called him that. You have only had him a few hours, boys. It will take him a day or two to learn his new surroundings and understand that his name is Silly. It might be better to play with him in a loose box where he can't escape until he is accustomed to you both.'

They nodded solemnly. 'We will do that, won't we, Tom? Are you going now? Your carriage isn't ready yet.'

'I have decided not to leave until Sultan is sound. I'm going down to the lake; would you like to come with me? I notice that there is a rowing boat and punt in the boathouse. I thought we could try one out together. But first you must inform your nursemaid. Remember, you must never go near the water on your own, even when you can both swim properly.'

They trotted off obediently and Gideon heard them talking to the nursemaid. Moments later they reappeared with her. 'I beg your pardon, my lord, but are you quite sure you want to go boating with these two little rascals?'

'I am quite sure, thank you. However, it might be wise if you accompanied us just in case you are needed.'

The girl looked relieved to be included in this jaunt and he didn't blame her. He was probably the last person she would wish to trust her precious charges with. He glanced at his smart apparel. 'Boys, I think we need to change into something that won't matter if it gets wet. If I remember correctly, the last time I was in a boat I returned extremely damp.'

There was no argument on this point, and they scampered off to change, leaving him to follow at a more stately pace. The boys would wait on the terrace if they were ready before him and vice versa. Ellis, his valet, wisely made no comment when he was asked to find garments that would not be ruined if immersed in lake water.

Gideon's appearance on the terrace in bare feet and shirtsleeves sent the children into fits of giggles. Immediately they sat down and stripped off their own stockings, boots and waistcoats.

'Now, lads, are you ready for your adventure?'

They frolicked around Gideon like a pair of overeager puppies, asking innumerable questions for which there were no sensible answers. What had possessed him to suggest this activity? He would have been better off taking them for a sedate walk through the woods.

It was cool and dark inside the boathouse, but light enough to see that the punt looked in better shape than the rowing boat. 'Right, the punt it is. Jump in, boys. No — let me rephrase that. Climb in very carefully. I have no wish for you to fall out so early in this escapade.'

He steadied the punt with one hand, and with the other carefully guided each child into the centre of the boat, where they sat quivering with excitement on the slightly damp and mouldy plush cushions.

Tom screwed up his face in puzzlement. 'How does this boat go, sir?

Where are the sticky-out things you have to pull and push to make it move?'

Gideon held up the punt pole. 'There are no oars, young man. I stand on this flat piece here and push us along with the pole.' They both looked unconvinced at his explanation. 'You will understand once we are underway. Hold tight; I cannot use it in here. I must move the punt out of the boathouse and then climb in myself.'

After a great deal of shoving and pushing, he eventually succeeded in his task. He carefully placed the long pole along the edge of the punt and scrambled onto the small wooden deck at the stern of the boat. The boys were sitting facing him and so far were quite dry. He doubted that would last for much longer, as he had not propelled a punt since his time at Oxford — and even then he had been the least proficient of his cronies.

'Right, I think we are finally ready to attempt to cross the lake. We must brave the shark-infested waters and pray we reach the island before we are capsized and eaten.'

He expected them to join in the play-acting, but for some extraordinary reason the boys believed what he said, even though they had been swimming quite safely in the water just the day before. Before he could prevent it, both of them jumped to their feet and attempted to climb onto the bank. The punt rocked alarmingly and the gap between the side and the bank got wider.

'Sit down. Tom, David, *sit down* or you will have us in the lake.'

The children were screaming. The thought of being plunged into waters that might be full of man-eating fish made them even more desperate to escape. Gideon's bare feet were already wet and he could not get a purchase on the slippery surface. He rammed the pole into the lake bottom and pushed with all his strength, praying he could prevent the boat from capsizing and himself from toppling into the water.

9

Sapphire was becoming increasingly frustrated at being trapped on a chaise longue whilst the sun was shining and her brothers and his lordship were outside enjoying themselves. The sound of their laughter carried quite clearly through the open window.

The window seat was no more than a few yards from where she was; she could hop such a short distance and would be able to elevate her foot just as well from there. She rang the bell and Jenny popped her head around the door.

'I want to be able to look at what's going on outside. If you give me your support, I can achieve that objective without placing my foot on the ground.'

She had barely got settled when she saw her brothers and their escort crossing the greensward towards the boathouse. She caught her breath. *He* had bare legs and feet, and his shirtsleeves were rolled up, exposing his muscular forearms. Tom and David were also without stockings and shoes. Meg was walking a respectful distance behind the three of them, her arms full of dry clothes and towels. This was going to be an interesting afternoon. Perhaps if she was very careful she could kneel on the window seat and rest her elbows on the windowsill. She would have a much better view like this. After a great deal of shuffling and wincing she was settled comfortably.

The trio had vanished into the boathouse and it was now impossible to see or hear what they were doing. Meg had found herself a place in the shade of the willow tree and sat down with her bundle. Ten minutes passed by before Sapphire spied the prow of the ancient punt emerging.

David and Tom were sitting facing the stern, and to her astonishment Lord

Ilchester was in the water and pushing the boat. Although the water was only two feet deep at the edge, his breeches would be submerged. Who would have thought it? The more she knew about this gentleman, the more he surprised her. With an athletic spring he landed on the punting platform and picked up the pole.

Her thoughts wandered as she watched this unusual spectacle. He would make an excellent father. She could not imagine another aristocratic gentleman prepared to get himself wet like this.

Then everything changed. Her brothers began to scream and stood up as if wishing to get out. The punt rocked alarmingly and the prow swung outwards, making it impossible for the boys to get off. Ilchester shouted at her brothers to sit down, but they ignored him. In desperation he rammed in the pole, swinging the boat towards the bank.

Too late! His feet slid from under

him and he disappeared head first into the lake. The impact sent the punt crashing into the bank and the children were hurled face first onto the grass. Sapphire's breath hissed through her teeth. What could have been a catastrophe was merely an amusing accident.

Meg was already at the children's side and they flung themselves into her arms, obviously beside themselves with terror. As the nursemaid was comforting them, Sapphire turned her attention to his lordship and was relieved to see him emerge from the deep.

She was now half-hanging out of the window, gazing wide-eyed with admiration. The wet white shirt clung to Gideon's shoulders. It was almost transparent, allowing her to see the breadth of his chest beneath the cloth.

'What is going on? What frightened the boys?' Her voice carried across the grass, and even from so far away he heard her. Only then did she remember his comment about her not yelling at him.

★ ★ ★

Dammit to hell! Gideon shook his head and spat out a mouthful of muddy water. This was supposed to have been a pleasurable experience, but he had made a complete nincompoop of himself as well as scaring the boys half to death. Thank God his last-minute effort to push the boat to the bank had been successful, and both children were safely in the arms of their nursemaid.

He was about to walk to the bank and climb out himself when someone shouted at him. The voice echoed across the park. Good grief! Sapphire had seen the debacle and was yelling at him from her sitting room on the first floor.

He could hardly get on his high horse when he was standing up to his knees in water and with his shirt clinging to him like a second skin. Instead of being irritated by her lack of decorum, he gave her a cheery wave. She was beckoning frantically and he mimed that he would come and see her after he had changed into something dry.

Firstly he must reassure the boys that the lake was not full of sharks. He squelched to the bank, vaulted out and then walked towards the boys, who had now stopped crying. The nursemaid tossed him a large towel and he nodded his thanks. He dropped to the grass beside them whilst he was drying his hair and face.

'What a pair of sillies you two are. Do you think that either your sister or I will take you anywhere near the lake if it *did* have sharks swimming around in it?' Now was not the time to explain where one would actually find these animals.

The boys exchanged glances and then stood up and pointed to the island. 'But you said — ' David began to say, but his brother interrupted him.

'Why did you say it if it was not true? Saffy says it's wrong to tell lies.'

'Do you never play at games of make-believe? Make a castle out of an upturned table and pretend you are knights of old fighting a dragon?'

They shook their heads. 'We play games with our toys,' Tom said, 'but we don't know how to do make-believe castles and pretend sharks. Will you show us, sir?'

Gideon was puzzled by this omission. Sapphire was a lively, intelligent young lady. Why had she not shown the boys how to use their imaginations? This was something he would ask her when he went to see her later on.

'Shall we have another go at getting to the island, boys? We are going to pretend there are dangerous fish trying to catch us, and you must look out and warn me if you see any.'

David still looked unsure about this notion of imaginary danger, but Tom immediately added his own twist to the tale. 'There are pirates out there too, and we are going to try and steal their treasure.' When his brother looked unsure, he leaned over and shoved him so hard he fell on his back. 'Don't be a silly, David. We are playing a game of let's pretend.'

David, not to be outdone, lashed out with his feet, and Tom joined him on the grass.

'What do you think you are doing, boys?' said Gideon. 'Get up immediately. There will be no further games today after such a display of bad manners.' He gestured to the nursemaid hovering nearby. 'Take your charges to their bedchamber. They will remain there for the rest of the day. I shall decide if they are to have any tea after I have spoken to Miss Stanton.'

The children looked so crestfallen at this sharp remark that he almost relented, then decided it would do them no harm to be disciplined. Boys had a tendency to fight, but the sooner they both learned to solve their differences with discussion, the better it would be for everybody.

The girl nodded to him before taking a snivelling child in each hand and marching them away. She obviously approved of his punishment. He glanced at the window, hoping their sister would not take exception to his interference.

However, she was no longer on the window seat, so either she had been so incensed by his actions she had not remained where she was, or she had missed the whole incident altogether.

Gideon met a gardener's boy on his way back. He had decided it would be better to go in through the side door rather than drip his way through the entrance hall, and instructed him to arrange for the punt and pole to be safely returned to the boathouse. If the children were still interested, he would take them out tomorrow after they had had their riding lesson.

Ellis was waiting, as always, to help him disrobe. His man commented dryly, 'How fortuitous, my lord, that you thought to put on your oldest garments.'

'It was indeed. I must now dress for a third time today, and have still to change into my evening rig at six o'clock.'

He had already spoken to the butler and asked if dinner could be served inside tonight, in the grand dining room. He had also requested a more formal meal, if possible, with several courses and removes. There was no point in dressing for dinner if the meal did not live up to the occasion.

As he was making his way to Sapphire's sitting room, it belatedly occurred to him that perhaps it had not been the wisest move to issue orders as if he were the master here. He hesitated outside the room. For the first time since he was a young boy, summoned to his father's study for a beating, he was nervous about knocking on a door.

★　★　★

'Jenny, Lord Ilchester will be along to see me as soon as he's changed into dry clothes. I don't want to be lounging on the daybed. Could you please assist me to the armchair?' When she explained to her maid what had just transpired, she

166

was not surprised at the reaction she received.

'Well I never did! What a to-do, I must say. If you will pardon me for saying so, miss, Lord Ilchester is not like any other lord I've ever met.'

Sapphire hid her smile — for, as far as she knew, Jenny had never met another aristocrat and neither had she, so they did not have the knowledge to make a comparison.

'I believe that, like my uncle, he prefers not to stand on ceremony. I'm sure he is an exception to the rule.' She hopped to the armchair, but before she sat she looked down at her simple muslin gown. 'I think I should change into something more elegant. Perhaps one of the new gowns that arrived the other day. The green muslin with capsleeves and the pretty embroidery around the hem would be ideal.'

It took longer than she'd expected, and she was forced to sit down twice during the procedure. She had barely taken her place in the high-backed padded armchair when there was a hesitant knock on the door. The last thing she wanted was another visitor just as Lord Ilchester was expected to arrive.

'Jenny, whoever it is, tell them I am not receiving at the moment.'

Her maid repeated her message and whoever it was did not argue and left quietly. 'Who was it?'

'Lord Ilchester. He looked most upset to be sent away.'

'I thought it was someone else come to bother me. Please, could you run after him and ask him to come back?'

Sapphire wished she could be the one to fetch him and try and explain away her unintended rebuff. A few moments later the door was pushed open and he stepped in. For the first time since she'd known him he looked uncertain; if she had not known better, she would have thought him actually nervous. He remained where he was and bowed. She could hardly get to her feet and respond with a curtsy.

'Please, come in and sit down. I will apologise, before you ask me to, for shouting like a fishwife across the park. I don't suppose you would believe me if I told you I have not shouted for any reason whatsoever since I was a little girl — that is until yesterday.'

His smile sent warm flutters through her chest and he strolled across to sit on the daybed — she noticed he had left the door wide open so propriety could not be said to have been breached.

'I gather from your maid's rather garbled message that you did not intend to send me away, you believed that I was someone else entirely? Were you expecting another visitor?'

Colour flooded Sapphire's cheeks. 'No, I wasn't, but I knew you were coming and did not want to be bothered with anyone else.'

His eyes sparkled with something she didn't recognise. 'In which case, my dear, I accept your apology.' He raised a hand as she drew breath to protest. 'Do not poker up. I know you have not apologised for sending me packing, but I'm sure you are about to.'

'You are quite impossible, sir. Now, tell me what caused the accident on the lake.'

When he had explained the whole, she detected some reservation in his demeanour. For a moment she was puzzled, and then realised he thought her a girl lacking in imagination; one who had denied her little brothers an interesting playtime.

'I think I must inform you, Lord Ilchester, that until my parents passed away a few months ago I had little to do with my brothers' upbringing. My time was spent tutoring local children in their letters and teaching them how to play the pianoforte. They were cared for by our mother when she was available and by the housekeeper when she was out.'

Her tone had been terse and he all but recoiled. 'I did wonder why they reacted so violently. We must ensure that in future they have plenty of opportunities to explore their imaginations.' He frowned and leaned towards her. 'Why on earth should a young lady of your impeccable pedigree have been obliged to spend their time in such a way?'

'My step-father had a limited income, and my father's pension ceased to be paid when Mama remarried. Therefore, without the added funds I brought in through my endeavours, we would have been unable to meet our expenses each month.' She was warming to her theme, which was something that had always irked her. 'You think that I enjoyed being separated from my little brothers? I love them and would do anything for them. However, earning a few shillings a week was of more use to them than teaching them to play imaginary games.'

He sat back, shaking his head as if displeased with her explanation. He was angry on her behalf. She wasn't sure she quite liked that idea. Neither, on reflection, was she happy at him including himself when talking about the education and upbringing of her brothers.

'My mother chose to elope with my father, and cut herself off entirely from her family. I doubt that Uncle John could have traced us, especially as she was now Mrs Palmer and not Mrs Stanton. But as far as I knew, there would have been little to inherit anyway as my maternal grandfather was a gambler and a profligate.'

'That is obviously a Bishop failing. Perhaps it's something that runs in the family, as my father was also that way inclined. I believe your grandfather was my great-uncle, so we are only tenuously related.'

'Some sort of cousins, several times removed. But you are a Bishop, and so is Uncle John.'

He sat back, shaking his head as if displeased with her explanation. Then he looked at her, his eyes blazing.

'Mr Bishop is to blame for the

situation you found yourself in. He made no push to find his sister after he returned to England. He might have known she would be in need of financial assistance.'

They chatted companionably for a further half an hour, and then Gideon rose and excused himself politely. 'I have yet to speak to Mr Bishop. It is quite possible he still thinks I have departed. You might also be a little surprised to discover I have requested that we dine formally tonight.' His smile was endearing, and she instantly forgave his high-handed interference in their lives.

'Whilst we are on the subject, my lord, I trust it was a slip of the tongue when you said that you were intending to be involved in a personal way in the upbringing of my brothers?'

His smile slipped and he looked a little shifty. There was something going on here and she did not like it one little bit. She smiled sweetly at him. 'Is there something you would like to tell me,

Lord Ilchester? Have you and my uncle been scheming behind my back?'

He shrugged and did not answer her question. 'I'm not at liberty to say what took place in a confidential conversation with Mr Bishop. You must speak to him yourself.' He raised an irritating eyebrow. 'Oh dear! Of course, you are unable to do so for two days at least. I shall return to collect you at six o'clock; I trust you will be ready by then?'

'Even incapacitated as I am, I do not require more than an hour to get ready. If you wish to speak to Uncle John you had better go immediately. He will not be expecting to have to change for dinner, and it takes him far longer than either you or I do.'

He jumped as if stabbed by a sharp hatpin and instantly became a formidable aristocrat. He gave her a fulminating stare. She must curb her tendency to issue requests that sounded like orders, for he obviously did not take kindly to them.

174

He nodded curtly and strode from the room, leaving her feeling a little deflated. She must do her best to be charming and conciliatory when he came to fetch her at six o'clock.

10

Sapphire stared at her bandaged ankle with dismay. 'There is no help for it, Jenny. I shall be obliged to go downstairs with no stocking or slipper on this foot. It hardly seems worthwhile putting anything on the other one, does it?'

'No stockings on at all, miss? I should think not! Whatever next? It's a good thing your evening gown is long, so it should cover your feet when his lordship carries you downstairs.'

'I have made other arrangements. Two of the new footmen are coming at a quarter to six to transport me to the dining room. I have no wish to be carried by Lord Ilchester. I suppose I should ask to be placed in the drawing room, but that would just complicate matters.'

The gown she had selected had a

dark golden silk underskirt covered by diaphanous sparkles, also in gold. Her hair had been dressed in a loose arrangement on top of her head and several russet curls framed her face. She tugged at the revealing neckline. 'I think this is far too low. Could you find me a *fichu* to tuck in? I do not wish to have quite so much bosom on display.'

'That would quite spoil the look of the gown, Miss Stanton. What about the pearl and topaz necklace with the matching ear bobs? That would look very pretty and cover up a lot of your front.'

When the jewellery was in place, Sapphire agreed with her maid. 'That looks much better. I am ready to go down, and I am sure I heard my escort arriving.'

With Jenny's arm firmly around her waist, she was able to hop smoothly into the sitting room. To her consternation, Lord Ilchester was waiting for her. He bowed.

'I heard that you were eager to be

down earlier than we planned, Miss Stanton, so here I am to take you.'

There was nothing she could do. This was a *fait accompli* and she had no option but to smile sweetly and accept his assistance. Her heart began to hammer as if it wished to escape from behind her overtight bodice and she dared not meet his eyes. The very thought of being held so close when there was so much of her flesh on display was quite unnerving.

'I had hoped to spare you the arduous task of carrying me about the place. However, as you are here, I am ready to depart. How did my uncle take the news that he had to dress for dinner tonight?'

'He was not unduly put out. In fact, he gave the appearance of being pleased. Now, shall we go?'

She wasn't quite sure of the etiquette involved when a young lady was about to be carried by a gentleman. Jenny remained supporting her until he moved to her side. 'Put your arm around my shoulder; that will make it much easier for me to lift you.'

She did as instructed, knowing that her fingers were trembling and her cheeks an unbecoming shade of scarlet. He muttered something impolite under his breath. 'Relax, sweetheart. I am not going to ravish you, merely carry you like a sack of potatoes to the drawing room.' He put one arm around her shoulders, and the other under her knees, and she was in mid-air.

Her nervousness was replaced by annoyance and instead of gripping his shoulder she grabbed hold of his immaculately tied neckcloth. How dare he refer to her as a sack of potatoes? Her grip tightened involuntarily.

'You are choking me,' he said. 'Kindly remove your hand from my stock and put it on my shoulder, or I shall dump you in the corridor and leave you to find your own way down.'

Immediately she stopped strangling him, as she was quite certain he would carry out his threat — he was not a gentleman to make false promises. 'I am sorry, my lord. My hold was quite inadvertent, I do assure you.' They both knew she was speaking falsehoods, but her words smoothed the matter over.

He strode along the spacious passageway and positively bounded down the stairs, jarring her ankle most painfully. She yanked on his stock. 'Put me down at once. I would prefer to hop the rest of the way rather than be mistreated by you.'

With studied care he did as she requested. 'I shall summon your footmen to carry you the rest of the way.' He didn't ask why she had made this demand; just stared at her through narrowed eyes before leaving her marooned halfway down the staircase.

She had two choices — to wait until the promised help arrived, or continue her journey on her derriere, which would be safe, but most undignified. She decided on the latter. It could be a considerable time before anyone was free to come to her aid, and she had no intention of standing on the staircase like a forgotten item.

After carefully lowering herself, she began her cautious descent. It was surprisingly easy and far less painful to travel this way than to be jounced and bounced by Lord Ilchester. She had reached the bottom step when Jarvis appeared with her uncle's bath chair. 'I thought as you would like a ride in this, Miss Stanton, seeing as his lordship saw fit to dump you on the stairs.'

This was hardly a respectful comment, but his sentiment was correct. 'Thank you. I don't know why I didn't think of it myself. I take it my uncle is already safely seated somewhere?'

'He managed with just one stick tonight, miss. I reckon he'll not need this for much longer. I hope I'll still have a position here after that.'

She edged into the bath chair before replying. 'Of course you will, Jarvis. This is a vast establishment and there is always room for a reliable and honest worker.'

Gideon regretted his actions before he had reached the drawing room, but he was damned if he was going to go back. He paused in front of a handsome gilt-framed mirror and viewed his mangled neckcloth with dismay. There was nothing for it; he would have to return to his room and replace it. Just as he was about to do so his host appeared in the doorway of the drawing room.

'Ah, there you are. What have you done with my niece?'

'She insisted she would prefer to be carried by the footmen as she originally arranged, so I have left her on the stairs and am about to go in search of them.'

The old man stared at his disarrangement and nodded. 'Probably wise, young man. I wish to speak to you. Don't concern yourself about your stock; there is no one to see it apart from family.'

There was no option but to follow his

host, who was, of course, immaculately turned out himself. Sapphire was wearing a stunning ensemble, an evening gown as fine as any he had seen in town. Despite his attraction to her, which was growing with every moment, he wasn't sure she would make him a suitable wife. He had never envisaged himself married to a young lady who contradicted him, gave him orders as if he were her lackey, and had an unfortunate tendency to screech like a fishwife.

Whether Sultan was sound or not, he would leave first thing tomorrow morning before he got further entangled and found himself pushed into a position where he was obliged to make her an offer. He would have to bring his family in three weeks' time, as he had already accepted the invitation, and he knew that his mother and sisters would be disappointed if he cancelled the visit.

Mr Bishop was moving remarkably well; he barely had need of the silver-topped cane he carried. Once they were comfortably ensconced, conversation began.

'I've been thinking about your offer to ride around my estates, my lord, and it would be most appreciated,' said John. 'After all, you will be responsible for keeping them in good heart once I am gone. My niece will have the right to remain here until she marries, but she will be unable to manage things herself. Society does not consider a female to have the wit to do so — which is patent nonsense, as I'm sure you will agree.'

'Indeed I do, sir, but the law thinks otherwise. However, it would make more sense for Miss Stanton to accompany the boys to Ilchester Abbey.' He frowned. This was not a conversation he wished to continue. 'However, I'm certain that by the time you do go to meet your Maker the point will be academic. The boys could well have reached their majority and my interference will not be required.'

Bishop chuckled into his glass. 'A kind thought, my boy, but my physician tells me otherwise. Outward appearances can be deceiving, you know.'

As Gideon was sipping his drink, he recalled that he had not sent word for anyone to fetch Sapphire. He shot to his feet just as Jarvis trundled her into the room in her uncle's strange conveyance. She ignored him and spoke solely to her uncle.

'See, Uncle John, I have my mobility returned to me thanks to your chair.' She waved away the servant who approached with a tray. 'I do not wish for any sherry wine. I have no taste for it.'

She chatted brightly about this and that as if Gideon were invisible. He was not used to being disregarded, especially by a chit of a girl. 'Miss Stanton, have you arranged for your return to your chamber later this evening?'

Slowly she swivelled in the chair and fixed him with a disapproving look. 'I shall certainly not be requiring your services, sir. Your cavalier approach to carrying me caused me a deal of pain and distress when you knocked my ankle against the wall on more than one occasion.'

It was as if he had been struck in the chest by a blow from a pugilist. Small wonder the poor girl had demanded to be set down. He had quite forgotten the reason he had been carrying her in the first place. 'Then my mangled neckcloth is well-deserved. We should have thought of conveying you in that contraption, as it is perfect for the job.' His previous ambivalence towards her began to dissipate. 'That is a beautiful gown; you look quite *ravisante*. My mama and sisters will be green with envy when they see it.'

The smile she bestowed on him melted the last of his reserve. He was as giddy as a schoolboy with his first crush, and knew himself to be in danger of falling in love with this enchanting girl. The rest of the evening spent in her company only reinforced his opinion.

The elaborate meal was served *à la française*, a cluster of dishes placed in the centre of the table for them to dip into as they chose. A small team of flunkies constantly removed plates they had tried and replaced them with different delicacies.

'I have never eaten anything like this in my entire life, Uncle John,' said Sapphire. 'I had no notion that Cook was so accomplished. There has been a prodigious amount of food, most of which we have barely touched. I am assuming the staff will enjoy it later.'

'An excellent repast, my dear, but a little too rich for my delicate digestion I fear.' Mr Bishop waved at the waiting footman and immediately he vanished to reappear moments later with Jarvis and the bath chair. 'If you will forgive me, I'm going to retire.'

Before Gideon could scramble to his feet, his host had hopped nimbly into the contraption and was whisked away, leaving him with Sapphire. The manoeuvre had taken place so quickly that he was convinced it had been prearranged in order to leave him alone with her.

Good gracious! thought Sapphire. Uncle John had winked at her as he vanished. Botheration! Unless Jarvis returned the bath chair, she would be obliged to rely on his lordship to return her to her room.

Her companion looked as annoyed as she was at this obvious manipulation by her uncle. Something prompted her to be open. 'I fear we have been set up, my lord. For some unfathomable reason my uncle is determined to push us together. I can assure you that I have no designs on you. You will not find yourself compromised in this house.'

This bold statement did not shock him as she had expected. Instead he raised his glass to her. 'I am well aware of how you feel about me, Miss Stanton, and I can assure you that I reciprocate your feelings.' With that cryptic comment he drained his glass of claret and got to his feet. 'Are you going to run away as well, or will you join me in the drawing room — perhaps outside on the terrace?'

She was tempted to agree, but this would entail being in his arms for far longer than she wished. Being held so close to him was unnerving, and she thought it would be wiser to cut the evening short. 'I would love to spend further time with you, but my ankle is throbbing unpleasantly and I think it would be best if I retired so that I might elevate it once more.' In fact she had quite forgotten her injury until that moment and, as if to punish her for her prevarication, she inadvertently knocked it against the leg of the chair. A shaft of agony made her flinch.

Gideon was on his feet in an instant and at her side, his face etched with concern. 'I am a brute to think of my own pleasure when you are in such pain. I shall return you to your apartment right away.' He lifted the chair with her in it with ease and then scooped her up. This time she was more relaxed and was happy to put her arm around his shoulder and rest her cheek against his jacket. For some reason he was tense, as if he disliked being so close to her.

Her journey was accomplished more smoothly this time as he made every effort not to jar her ankle. Although dinner had gone on for over two hours, the evening was still light, and she was too full to contemplate her bed just yet.

'Please place me on the chaise longue, my lord. I'm not retiring.'

He did so and then hastily stepped away. 'Goodnight, and thank you for your company; I cannot remember having spent a more pleasant evening.' He bowed, gave her one of his toe-curling smiles, and vanished.

Jenny helped Sapphire out of her evening gown and into her negligée, and she settled down with the latest novels that had arrived from Hatchards that very day. She finally went to her bed after ten o'clock, but found it difficult to sleep.

The more she considered it, the more she thought that her uncle was up to something. The only conclusion she could draw was that he wished her to marry Lord Ilchester. She turned over for the umpteenth time. That could not be the case, because if she did marry the handsome but impossibly autocratic gentleman, she would be obliged to leave Canfield Hall. Uncle John could not possibly wish her to do that, so his actions made no sense.

Her chest constricted and she fell back on the pillows in dismay when she realised what could be behind his actions. Was he dying and wished to make sure that she and the boys were taken care of? Once this thought was in her head she could not rest until she had confirmed it one way or the other.

The overmantel clock had struck midnight some time ago. Everybody would be asleep, but she was determined to make her way downstairs even if it meant making the journey on her bottom or her knees. If her beloved uncle was indeed at his last prayers, she wished to know about it now and could not wait until the morning.

11

Sapphire swung her legs to the floor and then, still holding on to the bedpost, stood up, waiting for her injured ankle to fold under her. It was a trifle sore, but hardly hurt at all even when she walked normally. She could hardly go gallivanting around the house in her diaphanous negligée, but she wasn't going to go to the bother of getting dressed either.

She found the black silk domino that she had ordered to wear over an evening gown if she should ever wish to go out at night. This would be ideal, as the voluminous folds covered her from neck to toe. There was little point in wearing a bedroom slipper on one foot only, so she decided to go as she was.

It was going to be impossible to carry a candlestick as well as lean on the wall and keep her skirts from beneath her feet. The shutters and curtains had not been drawn in her sitting room and she could see there was a full moon tonight. She would just have to pray there was sufficient illumination coming in from the windows. Fortunately this was the case, and she was able to find her way along the passageway without too much difficulty.

By the time she was halfway down the staircase she was bitterly regretting her impulsive decision. The ankle that had seemed almost recovered ten minutes ago was now no longer able to bear her weight. She sunk down and completed her descent on her backside.

The distance to her uncle's apartment was as far again as she had come, and she doubted she could complete the journey without mishap. This was ridiculous — she was not going to give up so easily. A vast expanse of chequered tiles stretched in front of her; how was she going to negotiate this with no wall to help her balance?

What she needed was a walking stick

or something similar, but where was she to get such a thing? Then she spied a container made from an elephant's foot which contained several canes and sticks. She thought she could hop as far as that without too much difficulty.

She withdrew two canes, and once her weight was taken by these, the pain in her ankle eased. The only disadvantage with this method of travel was that she was making far too much noise. If the passageways were carpeted, not only would it be warmer, but it would have made her progress quieter.

After a deal of clumping and shuffling, she eventually reached her destination and was unsurprised to find her uncle's valet, his nightshirt collar clearly visible above his black jacket, waiting to receive her.

'Good evening, miss. The master is awake.' Like a magician he produced the bath chair, and with a sigh of relief she tumbled into it.

'I'm sorry to have woken you, but I have something of the utmost urgency to discuss with my uncle and it could not possibly wait until the morning.' There had been no need to give any explanation, but they stood on no ceremony at Canfield Hall.

She was pushed through the small drawing room and directly into her uncle's chamber, where he was sitting up in bed, his nightcap set at a jaunty angle. He did not seem at all put out by her nocturnal visit.

'Come in, my dear girl. I am eager to know what prompted you to hobble all this way.'

Once they were alone she studied him closely for any telltale signs of fatal illness, but could see nothing untoward. 'Why are you throwing Lord Ilchester and me together in this way? The only possible explanation, as far as I can see, is that you are anticipating your demise and wish to see me settled before you depart.' She gave him no opportunity to answer but continued, fixing him with a basilisk stare. 'You look perfectly healthy to me, thank the good Lord, so what game are you playing with us?'

He looked a little sheepish, but unrepentant. 'There is no pulling the wool over your eyes, my dear. I am perfectly well — indeed I would like to live for years. However, it is possible that I could be struck down with a fatal seizure at any time. That was what laid me low in the first place.'

Her eyes filled and she reached out to clasp his hand. 'How is that possible? You said that you suffered your first seizure more than five years ago and have had none since. Is that not a sign that you will not have another one?'

'These things are in the hands of the Lord. I could live healthily for another twenty years or could meet my maker tomorrow. Please, my dear child, do not look so stricken. I am merely stating the truth, and it is better that you know it.'

She swallowed the lump in her throat with difficulty. 'I understand that you wish to know that you leave me taken care of, but I have no intention of marrying Lord Ilchester, as I wish to remain here and take care of my brothers.'

'I fear that you cannot be their guardian if I am gone, as the law does not recognise the authority of an unmarried woman. Therefore, I have changed my will so that David and Thomas will be the wards of Lord Ilchester, and he will manage the estate until they reach their majority.'

'Am I also to be part of his inheritance?'

'We discussed that very point, but decided you were old enough to take care of your own finances without his assistance. You will be a very wealthy young woman, and have the right to remain at Canfield Hall until you choose to reside elsewhere.' He paused and yawned widely. 'I am sure you understand, child, that Lord Ilchester might well prefer to have the boys with him and not leave them here in your care.'

'He would take them away over my dead body, Uncle John. If anything happens to you, and God forbid that it does, then we will all remain here where we are happy. Ilchester can take it or leave it.'

The strange remarks his lordship had made earlier were now explained. He already knew he would be involved with her brothers' upbringing and had been staking his claim. There was no point in arguing the issue; the matter had been settled and there was nothing she could do about it.

'I shall leave you to sleep, Uncle John, and return to my own bed. If your valet would be so kind as to push me back to the stairs I believe I can manage to complete the rest of the distance myself.'

'There is no need to do that, Miss Stanton. I have been summoned to offer my assistance.' Lord Ilchester took hold of the handles of the bath chair, and before she could complain, she was whisked out into the passageway and across the entrance hall.

They had travelled at such a speed it

took her a moment to catch her breath. 'What are you doing here? How did you know you were needed?' She now had time to study him more carefully and saw to her horror that he was wearing only his breeches and shirt — the latter hanging loose around his knees and open almost halfway down his broad chest. The very idea of being held by him was unsettling.

'You are inappropriately dressed, sir, and I have no wish to be carried by you. That would be quite unacceptable.'

'Believe me, sweetheart, you are calling the kettle black. Now, do not make a fuss, there's a good girl. I wish to return to my bed as soon as I may.'

She gripped the edges of the flimsy domino across her bosom in the vain hope that she had not revealed too much of herself. Obediently she held out her arms, and he picked her up with as much interest as if he were transporting a sack of flour.

They ascended the stairs as if his shirt tails were on fire, and before she could draw breath she was in her own bedchamber and being unceremoniously dumped onto the centre of the bed. There was no time to thank him for his gallantry, if his careless approach to the matter could be called that, as he was gone in a flash of white and she was alone.

Dammit to hell! Gideon thanked God he had not had the time to dress correctly. Fortunately the shirt flapping around his knees had served to cover his embarrassment. When he had been woken and asked to come at once to Mr Bishop's apartment he had feared the worst — that the old man had suffered a second seizure.

He had not wasted time dressing, just dragged on his breeches and thrown his shirt over his head before thundering down, only to find he had been summoned to carry Sapphire back to her bedroom. What the devil she was doing downstairs in the middle of the night he had no idea — but seeing her in her nightwear was almost his undoing.

She was surely the most beautiful and desirable girl in the kingdom. His pulse was pounding through his body as he recalled the sweet curve of her bosom and her glorious copper curls tumbling around her shoulders. Unless he removed himself immediately from Canfield Hall he would do something he might live to regret. He had only known the girl for a couple of days, and this was no basis to make a decision that would change his life forever.

He would wake his man and get him to pack immediately. It would be dawn in a couple of hours and he wanted to be on his way by then. Such an abrupt departure might well give offence, and that would be unpardonable. Possibly a letter written to both Mr Bishop and Sapphire would smooth things over. He would write these notes whilst he waited to leave.

In the letter to his host he offered no explanation; just apologised for leaving so early. He also said he was looking forward to coming back with his family for the house party next month. After three attempts he gave up the notion of writing to Sapphire. He scarcely knew her, and leaving her a personal message might well cause her unnecessary distress. After all, she had made it abundantly clear she had no wish to leave her uncle for anybody, however eligible they might be.

As he had only one item of luggage, his valet was quite happy to carry that himself, thus disposing of the need to summon a sleepy footman to assist. Gideon was tempted to creep out like a thief in the night, but his dignity would not allow him to do so. Dressed immaculately in his dark green jacket, grey-silk waistcoat and Hessians, so well-polished one could see one's face in them, he was ready to face the world. He marched through the house and waited whilst the butler hastily unlocked the front door to allow him to exit. The carriage was not yet outside, so he strolled around to the stable, where he met the head groom.

'The horses are being put to, my lord. You should be able to depart very soon. I fear that your stallion is not ready to be ridden.'

'Then I shall leave him in your good care, Ned, and collect him when I come back for Miss Stanton's celebration. Turn him out; it will do him good to graze outside for a while.'

The man touched his cap and grinned. 'He's taking a mighty fine interest in Miss Stanton's grey mare. Would you have any objection if we ran them together in the meadow?'

'A good idea. Any progeny from such excellent stock would be well worth seeing.'

His coachman had completed harnessing the matching bays that drew his barouche, and so Gideon climbed in the vehicle without bothering to open the door or use the step. Being an open vehicle, it was ideal for a summer drive through the countryside, though less pleasant in the winter months.

The carriage halted outside the front of the building in order to allow Gideon's manservant to join the coachman on the box after stowing the portmanteau under the seat. 'Find somewhere pleasant to break our journey, Higgins. The horses will need to be watered and fed, and so shall we.'

The coachman raised his whip. 'I reckon it'll take just over four hours to return to Ilchester Abbey, my lord, so I'll stop after two.' With no further ado, the man released the brake and snapped his whip in the air, and the carriage moved smoothly away down the drive.

★　★　★

Sapphire was impatient to resume her normal life. With a walking stick she was quite sure she would be able to hobble about quite satisfactorily. However, Dr Smith was due to visit this morning, and she thought it sensible to wait until she had his opinion on the matter.

There had been no sign of the boys so far; they must be having their riding lesson with Lord Ilchester. His given name was Gideon — did she dare to use it in the privacy of her head? She had scarcely touched her breakfast tray. Her normally healthy appetite appeared to have deserted her.

The book she had found so interesting yesterday now failed to hold her attention. Why did no one come to see her? Then there was the sound of running footsteps in the passageway outside her sitting room, and she knew her brothers had arrived to visit at last. She could hardly ask Jenny or the chambermaid what was going on downstairs, but she could certainly draw the information from the children.

'Come in, boys. Did you enjoy your lesson? Was Lord Ilchester pleased with you?'

They scrambled onto the daybed, both eager to sit beside her, and quite forgetting that she had an injury to her ankle. 'Ned and Billy did it, Saffy. His lordship has gone home. Billy says he left without his breakfast,' Tom announced.

'I see. I thought he was to stay until Sultan was ready. Surely he did not take the stallion with him?'

David tugged at her sleeve. 'No, and it's ever so exciting. Ned says Star and Sultan are going to have a baby horse next year.'

This was news indeed. She held her breath, waiting for one of them to ask how this miracle would take place, but fortunately they had other interesting news to impart and did not require her to explain how Mother Nature worked. She was aware of the mechanics of the action between animals, and presumably humankind as well, but had no clear idea how this actually took place. Mama had never got round to telling her, and now it was too late.

Her mind wandered as the children chatted on about swimming lessons and riding lessons and picnics. The act of love required the husband and wife to remove their clothes — that much she was sure of; and it took place in the privacy of the bedchamber. After that her knowledge was sketchy, and she wished she had somebody she could ask. An image of Gideon in a transparent shirt which clung to his manly torso filled her head with unexpected thoughts.

'Saffy, Saffy, you are wool-gathering. We asked if you were going to come down today after Dr Smith has come.'

'I beg your pardon, David. I did not sleep well last night. I have every intention of joining you in the garden later. Even if I can't play, I can watch you do so. Perhaps Uncle John will allow some of the boys an hour or so off, so you can have another game of rounders, or perhaps cricket this time?'

'We can push you in the bath chair. Uncle said we can as he doesn't need it anymore. All you have to do is get downstairs.' Tom pointed at the two walking sticks leaning drunkenly against the far wall. 'Are those for you to walk with?'

She nodded. 'Yes, my ankle is so much better I am sure I can manage with those to lean on.'

Dr Smith pronounced her well enough to leave the daybed but warned her against overtaxing herself, as this could lead to permanent damage to the ankle. Reluctantly she agreed to be wheeled around by her brothers, and they thought this was a lark.

Uncle John was reclining on a comfortable armchair, his feet on the padded footstool, in the shade of a spreading oak tree on the lawn. He seemed remarkably pleased to see her.

'Your young man has departed. However, he left me a gracious note thanking me for my hospitality and confirming that he and his family will be coming to our house party to celebrate your twentieth name day. How are the arrangements progressing, my dear?'

The rest of the day passed swiftly and there was no time to think about Gideon, or why he had left without saying goodbye — indeed, why he had left before everybody was up. She would ask him when he came, if she got the opportunity to speak to him alone.

Everything was in hand for the garden party, and she was confident the housekeeper, the butler and estate manager were quite capable of arranging matters from now on. Invitations had been written to their neighbours and these would be delivered over the next day or two. If they were accepted, it would mean that two other families would be staying at Canfield Hall alongside the Ilchesters. Sapphire was eagerly anticipating being able to meet some young ladies of her own age. There were three girls accompanying their parents — and two gentlemen.

Once her ankle was fully restored, she intended to make sure her brothers were competent swimmers. She had also given instructions that the punt and both the rowing boats should be inspected and refurbished so they would be available to any of the guests who might wish to use them.

The croquet lawn was being carefully tended by the head gardener, and the necessary equipment to play a game of cricket had been discovered in the attic. She and her uncle were discussing this after dinner a week after Lord Ilchester had gone.

'I have watched a cricket match once before, Uncle, and it was most agreeable. Do you think we might have an impromptu match between Canfield Hall and the village? There is to be a tug of war, so why not a cricket match?'

'An excellent notion. I shall speak to Jarvis. He has little to do now that I am more mobile, so organising this will keep him busy.'

'Will our house guests take part, do you think?'

'Absolutely. I shall appoint Lord

Ilchester as captain. He seems like an athletic man.'

An image of this gentleman filled her head and she nodded in agreement.

12

Gideon had ample time on his return journey to consider his options with regard to his emotional entanglement with Sapphire. At eight-and-twenty, he must be considered more than ready to set up his nursery with a suitable young lady. Mama had already suggested several likely candidates amongst the latest crop of debutantes, though none of them had stirred his senses in a way that Sapphire had.

After enjoying a leisurely and tasty breakfast he returned to the barouche. He stretched his legs across the well of the carriage and, closing his eyes, enjoyed the feel of the June sunshine on his face. Sapphire was not the sort of young lady he had envisaged marrying — not that he had given the matter a great deal of thought up until this point. Somehow he had always supposed he would select a dainty, blonde, quiet, well-mannered girl who would make an excellent mother, whilst allowing him to be the master in his own home.

How had a young lady who was so different from his expectations stolen his heart? Sapphire was above average height, and rounded in all the necessary places, with vibrant chestnut hair. She was certainly not quiet or well-mannered, and if he married her he would be constantly challenged. She was as far from submissive and obedient as any woman in the kingdom. But he knew, without a shadow of a doubt, that no other would do for him.

The carriage rocked alarmingly as one wheel dropped into a pothole, and this jerked him from his reverie. His coachman called a cheery apology from the box and the journey continued. Gideon realised they were already trundling through his land — he would be home within the hour.

One thing was for certain: he must

not let his family know he had decided to marry Sapphire Stanton. It was going to take a deal of wooing and sweet-talking to convince the lady in question that she was ready to give up her freedom. She would protest about leaving Canfield Hall, but he could put in a tenant who would take care of the place until the boys were old enough to live there on their own. Mr Bishop would also come to Ilchester Abbey and join the family; the place was more than big enough to accommodate a dozen extra residents and still have room to spare.

Satisfied with his decisions, he hastily checked that his neckcloth was neatly arranged and his Hessians spotless, and that there was no dust or debris on his immaculate topcoat. During the next three weeks he must review his home and see what needed updating, with a view to bringing his bride and her family to live there. Not a man to procrastinate, he was determined to make Sapphire an offer whilst at the house party, and intended to arrange his nuptials before the end of the year.

That she would most definitely object to his suggestion did not deter him in the slightest. When he made up his mind he always achieved his objective, and he was sure that persuading the woman he loved to distraction to marry him would be a simple and enjoyable matter.

★ ★ ★

The day finally dawned for the arrival of the first of the house guests. Indeed, their baggage and servants were already present. Sapphire was making a final tour of inspection with the house-keeper, Mrs Banks. 'The house is almost unrecognisable from the one I arrived at a few months ago. Everything is sparkling, freshly painted and refurbished.'

'It does you credit, Miss Stanton, to have organised everything so quickly. As you know, I've been here since Mr

Bishop bought the place, but it has never looked its best until now.' Mrs Banks opened the door to the fourth guest apartment. 'I am putting Sir Joshua and Lady Jamieson in here, miss, and their two young ladies in the chamber next to them.'

'I have no need to inspect anywhere else, Mrs Banks. I am delighted with everything I have seen this morning. I believe Lord Ilchester and his party will be the first to arrive; they should be here by mid-afternoon. Then you must expect Sir Joshua and Lady Jamieson and their daughters, and lastly the Forsyth family. I am glad that their two sons are to accompany them or we would be desperately short of gentlemen. As they have the furthest to travel, they might not be here until just before dinner time, so Cook must be prepared to delay things if necessary.' Mr and Mrs Forsyth were acquaintances of her uncle, but he had not seen them for some time. They had not been on the list that Gideon had left.

As she was returning to the ground floor her brothers appeared, smelling distinctly of the stables, with their nursery maid in tow. 'We can ride properly now, Saffy,' said David. 'Ned says we can go with you next time you take Star out.'

'That is excellent news, boys. I'm sure Lord Ilchester will be impressed by your progress. I am going to check the boathouse and the boats, and look at the new jetty that has been built. Do you wish to come with me?'

'Yes please,' Tom said, hopping from one foot to the other. 'Now we can swim properly, can we go down to the lake by ourselves?'

'Absolutely not. However, you may go if Meg is with you, but you must not take a boat out or go in the water unless I am there.' Although they were both confident swimmers, until they were older and had developed more than a doggy-paddle to propel themselves along, she wasn't allowing them to swim unsupervised.

The boathouse had been lime-washed and scrubbed, and the two rowing boats and punt had been varnished and fresh upholstery put in place. Satisfied everything was perfect, Sapphire returned to the house. 'You must go upstairs and wash and change, boys. I want you spotless and on your best behaviour when our guests arrive.'

It was a shame that none of their visitors were bringing any younger children with them. Uncle John had explained that parents generally left their youngest progeny in the care of their nannies and nursemaids when making visits — only adult children accompanied them.

'Tomorrow will be much more fun for you both. You have my permission to help with setting up the outside events for my name day garden party. There will be a hog roast, a tug of war, a cricket match, and a Punch and Judy show.'

'Tom said there will be stilt-walkers

and fire-eaters too, Saffy. Are they going to come?'

'I sincerely hope so. They are definitely booked. And as it is such a special occasion, you will be allowed to remain up until dark to watch the fireworks and the dancing. The only thing that could spoil the event is if it rains.'

Tom pointed to the marquee that had been erected for this eventuality. 'We can go in that big tent if it's wet, and anyway we don't mind the rain, do we, David?' His twin agreed, and they ran off chattering about everything they intended to do tomorrow.

Sapphire found her uncle relaxing on the terrace reading the newspaper. 'How are you, my dear girl? You look positively blooming — all this excitement is obviously agreeing with you.' He waved towards a chair and she took it willingly.

'I am so looking forward to it. Thank you so much for allowing me to have such an extravagant party when it is not even my majority I'm celebrating — becoming twenty years of age is neither here nor there. However, I must own to be a little nervous about having such prestigious house guests here. Remember, Uncle John, I have never mixed in society before.'

He snorted and shook his head. 'Stuff and nonsense, my girl. My sister was gentry and she will have brought you up properly. You have pretty manners, lively conversation and excellent deportment. There will not be a more beautiful, intelligent or eligible young lady present at your party.'

She stared open-mouthed at this unexpected praise. 'Uncle John, thank you for your compliments, but I believe you are a trifle biased. And please do not mention that word again — I am not *eligible*. I have no intention of getting married in the foreseeable future as I could not be happier than I am now. Why should I give up everything I have here to start again somewhere else which might not be nearly as pleasant?'

He chuckled, but did not look convinced by her statement. 'You say that now, my dear, but when you meet the right gentleman and fall in love, your tune will change — I guarantee it.' His smile faded and he reached out and took her hand with a surprisingly strong grip. 'You know how things are with me, and if you want to make me happy you will do as I ask and think about the future. The doctor said that worry and stress could aggravate my condition and I'm sure that you do not wish to do that. Knowing that you will be taken care of when I'm gone is all I want.'

It was impossible to withstand this plea, even though he was using his ill health to manipulate her into agreeing to something she had no wish to do. 'Very well. I give you my word that if I, by some miracle, meet the gentleman I wish to spend the rest of my life with, I will not let my personal feelings about leaving Canfield Hall stand in the way.'

'Thank you, Sapphire. You have made

my old heart glad.' He definitely had a smug expression as he sat back and hid his face in his news journal.

She watched him fondly for a few minutes, and then patted his arm and left him to read. Although he had manoeuvred her into a corner, on reflection she considered she was still at liberty to do as she promised and still remain with him and the boys at Canfield Hall. She would never marry without there being love on both sides — therefore, any gentleman who wished to marry her would naturally agree to live at Canfield. After all, would it not be his intention to fulfil her every wish?

There was little left for her to do apart from change into something more elegant before the first guests arrived. She glanced at the tall clock in the drawing room and saw that there was at least another hour before she had to return to her chamber to get changed. She would walk through the woods, where it would be cool and pleasant under the green canopy. There was no necessity to inform anyone of her plans, as she would not be gone long and every member of staff was busy about their designated tasks. Therefore, she retied the bow on her chip straw bonnet more securely and set off across the grass to the inviting shade of the trees.

After she had been walking for a while, she heard a strange cry and froze, before recovering her equilibrium when she recognised the sound as that of an animal in pain. The pitiful cry was coming from somewhere deep within the undergrowth and, ignoring the damage to her gown, she pushed her way forwards.

'My goodness! You poor thing. Don't worry, I shall soon have you free.' Her comforting words appeared to soothe the matted creature spread-eagled on the ground. It was a dog of indeterminate ancestry and medium size. Somehow the unfortunate beast had become entangled in a bramble bush and, from the look and smell of it, had been there for some time.

'There there, Saffy will soon have you free. Keep still, there's a good dog. It is going to take me a little while to remove the briars, for they are quite embedded in your shaggy coat.'

Fortunately she was wearing gloves this morning, something she did not always bother to do, and these were helping to protect her hands as she carefully removed each strand of the vicious thorns. The dog licked her hand and his tail wagged a little, although he was too weak to do more than that.

By the time the animal was free Sapphire was filthy, her dress quite ruined, and her arms severely scratched. However, this was of no matter to her, as she was more concerned about rescuing the unfortunate creature and carrying him back to the house to be treated.

Eventually he was free, and she sat back on her heels and encouraged him to stand. He made a valiant effort but his legs collapsed under him each time.

'There is nothing for it, my boy; I shall have to carry you.' She glanced ruefully at her dishevelled state and then smiled. 'It is too late to worry about my appearance — this gown is quite beyond repair — so a little more grime and blood will be of no moment.'

The animal was surprisingly heavy, and it took her several attempts to grasp him securely and then regain her feet. Although not a particularly large dog, he was somewhat bigger than she had anticipated. Slowly she reversed through the brambles and undergrowth until she had regained the path. The noxious odour coming from the wretched animal made her eyes water. No doubt he was riddled with vermin and she would need to burn her clothes. 'There is no point in worrying about that, young man; I am beyond redemption. I shall carry you straight to the stables and oversee your bath myself. After that, and a good meal, I am sure you will be on the road to recovery.'

She prayed this was actually the case. She knew little about canines; her brothers' was the first she had had any dealings with. She paused to catch her breath when she regained the path. It would probably be sensible to take the longer route and thus arrive at the stable yard from the tradesmen's entrance.

'I fear I must go back the way I came, Shaggy, and risk being seen by the workmen in the park preparing for tomorrow. I hope I am strong enough to get you back safely.'

★ ★ ★

Gideon regretted his decision to travel inside the carriage with his mother and sisters within an hour of leaving Ilchester Abbey. The girls chatted constantly and his head was ringing with their silliness.

'Please, Elizabeth, I have told you a dozen times that I am not sure who will be at Canfield Hall,' he said. 'I supplied Mr Bishop with a list of names and addresses, but have no notion if he invited all or none of them.'

His mother smiled at his sharp tone. 'There is no need to be snippy, Gideon. Your sisters are just curious to know who they will be mixing with over the next week.'

He was well aware that his siblings were constantly on the lookout for eligible partners. They were due to make their come-out next year, but he was certain they would be happy to find themselves a titled and wealthy husband before then. Fortunately Henry, away at school, was like him and was more interested in a person's character than their pocketbook.

Elizabeth — he only knew it was she because Mama had told him this sister would be wearing pink ribbons on her bonnet, whereas Emily had green — smiled sunnily. 'Mama, it matters not who is there; Emily and I are going to have a splendid time. This is our first house party, and we are determined to enjoy it.'

Emily agreed. 'I do hope there will be dancing. Not a formal ball, of course — we are not out yet — but it would be perfectly proper for us to dance informally, would it not, Mama?'

Gideon's mother glanced at him. 'Of course it would, my love, if your brother agrees. However, I doubt there will be sufficient people to make up a set. I wish you knew more about this event, Gideon, for I am beside myself with curiosity.'

'I'm well aware of that, Mama. Indeed, you would not have dragged us off so early this morning otherwise. You do realise we are going to arrive long before the appointed time? Don't be surprised if we find things in disarray.' He pulled out his pocket watch and flicked open the case. He had said they would be arriving mid-afternoon, when in fact it would be barely midday.

The coach slowed to negotiate the turn into the drive of Canfield Hall. Gideon was as eager as his family to reach their destination. Sapphire had been constantly in his thoughts and he could not wait to see her again.

Elizabeth and Emily, despite their desire to be considered adults, were craning out of the windows like urchins, and Gideon was about to reprimand them when Emily screeched most unbecomingly.

'Look at that! I've never seen anything like it. Mama, Gideon, there's a filthy village girl with red hair down her back walking towards the house.'

'She's carrying a dog. Why should she be going to Canfield Hall?' Elizabeth added.

Gideon was on his feet and had lifted Elizabeth from his path before she had finished her sentence. He shouted to the coachman to halt, had the door open before the vehicle was stationary, and jumped out. Sure enough, he saw Sapphire stumbling towards the house carrying an injured animal. She must have heard them but didn't stop or look round.

'Miss Stanton, wait — let me help

you.' He was beside her in a few strides and almost gagged at the stench emanating from the animal. Wearily she raised her head, and he was horrified to see her beautiful skin was marred by scratches and her arms in an even worse state. 'Here, sweetheart, let me take the beast.'

'No, there is no need for both of us to ruin our garments. I am quite capable of carrying him to the stables, thank you, my lord.

To his astonishment his mother arrived at their side. 'Here, Miss Stanton, I have a rug. If Gideon wraps the dog in that, he will avoid ruining his clothes.'

Sapphire's smile was breathtaking beneath the blood and grime. 'Thank you, my lady, and I apologise for being seen like this. But I could not leave this poor animal to die in the woods.'

'Of course you could not, my love. I would have done the same.'

Gideon almost choked. The thought of his immaculate mama risking her

ensemble in such a way was unthink-
able. 'Here, I have the rug ready,' he
said. 'Let me take him now, Miss
Stanton.'

The transfer was completed successfully and Gideon's mother returned to
the carriage, leaving him alone with
Sapphire. 'I cannot tell you how
relieved I am that you are here to carry
the poor thing,' she said. 'He is far
heavier than I anticipated. I shall
accompany you to the stables and then
will minister to the animal myself, for I
could not be any dirtier than I am
already.'

'You shall do no such thing, sweetheart. There are perfectly good stable
lads who can do the job. You must
return at once to the house and get
yourself clean and your scratches seen
to.'

'I suppose you are correct, my lord.
This is not how I anticipated meeting
your family. Your mama, Lady Serena,
must be the most understanding person
in the county. I cannot imagine anyone

else being so kind to me in the circumstances.'

'We are unpardonably early, so if there is fault, it is on our side.'

'Everything is ready, apart from myself. If you're quite sure, my lord, that you can do what is necessary for the well-being of this animal, then I shall slip in the side door and hope I meet nobody else.'

She vanished along a narrow path, leaving him to carry the wretched animal to the stables. Within less than a quarter of an hour everything was arranged, and the dog was perfectly content to be abandoned by his rescuers. Gideon checked his own appearance and sniffed his jacket sleeve. Thankfully the smell had not permeated through the rug and he had no necessity to change.

The baggage cart would have arrived yesterday afternoon along with his valet, his mother's abigail and his sisters' dresser. He took the path that led directly to the house and entered through the side door as if he were a member of the household. His mouth curved at the thought. At the moment he was the most senior member of the Bishop family, but he hoped that by the end of the visit he would be Miss Stanton's betrothed.

13

In less than half an hour Sapphire was bathed, changed, and her hair correctly dressed. The guest wing was on the far side of Canfield Hall, so she had no notion if Lord Ilchester and his family were upstairs or down.

'Jenny, I must go. I am sure I look as well as I am going to, so no further primping and fussing will make any difference.'

Her maid curtsied. 'You should have the doctor to attend to your scratches, miss. One or two are very deep and nasty-looking.'

'You have cleaned them splendidly; they hardly hurt at all. As I am wearing a long-sleeved gown, the damage to my arms is no longer visible. There is nothing I can do about my face, but I'm sure nobody would be uncivil enough to comment.'

She had dallied too long upstairs; she was the hostess and should have been available to see that her guests were settled comfortably. There was also the matter of the dog, and she could not relax until she was sure he was going to make a full recovery.

The guest wing and the family wing conjoined at the gallery, but there was no sign of visitors in the wide passageway. They must be either in their apartments or somewhere downstairs in one of the reception rooms. She was about to descend when Gideon strode into sight. Her heart skipped a beat. Gathering up her skirts, she hurried down the staircase and followed him across the hall and into the drawing room. He must have heard her, as he was waiting just inside the doors.

'Before you ask me, the foundling is doing well. I'm sure that in a few days he will be completely restored, and then you will have to decide what to do with him.'

It was hard to form a sensible reply

when he was smiling at her like that. 'Thank you, I am relieved to hear you say so. I shall keep him, of course. He will be good company for Silly — I know, calling a puppy that is ridiculous, but it is what my brothers chose.'

'In which case, I have the perfect name for your new pet. Call him Smelly or possibly Stinky.'

'I have already named him, sir. He is to be called Shaggy. Now, I wish to be formally introduced to Lady Serena and your sisters. Are they down?'

'The girls are exploring the grounds, and my mother is with your uncle. They were having an animated conversation when I excused myself a while ago.'

Sure enough, her ladyship was sitting beside Uncle John on the terrace and they appeared to have struck up a cordial relationship already. Lady Serena jumped to her feet and rushed across with outstretched arms to greet Sapphire.

'My dear Miss Stanton, you're looking quite enchanting. I cannot tell you how glad I am that you invited me to your name day celebrations. Mr Bishop has been explaining what you have planned to entertain us.'

Sapphire had been going to curtsy but found herself embraced and roundly kissed on both cheeks. 'We are delighted to have you here, my lady. I hope your accommodation is to your liking.'

'Everything about this house is to my liking, my dear, and your little brothers are quite sweet. They are showing my daughters the boathouse.' She waved airily towards the lake. 'There, I can see them all. I hope Elizabeth and Emily have the sense to keep your brothers away from the water, for you can be very sure neither of my girls would dream of going in after them.'

'They can both swim, Mama, so in the unlikely event of them tumbling in they would be quite able to rescue themselves,' Gideon said.

The butler glided through the French doors and bowed. 'A cold collation is set out in the small dining room, Miss

Stanton, whenever your guests should wish to avail themselves of it.'

'Thank you, Robinson. We will come through soon.' She turned to Lady Serena and her uncle. 'If you will excuse me, I shall walk down to the lake and bring everyone back for luncheon.'

'I shall accompany you, Miss Stanton,' Gideon offered. 'After being cooped up in a carriage for hours with my sisters, I crave fresh air and silence.'

Once they were out of earshot, he spoke again. 'I'm surprised you did not yell for them to return, my dear. I can assure you I heard you perfectly when you shouted from your sitting room last time I was here.'

She ignored his playful remark. He had said he wished to enjoy the silence, and who was she to go against his wishes? But he was having none of this.

'Miss Stanton,' he began, and his tone was not encouraging, 'I am not accustomed to being ignored.'

'Then enjoy the new experience, my lord. I'm sure you will get used to it in time.' She could not keep back her giggle and, not waiting for his response, she picked up her skirts and prepared to run the remaining distance to the boathouse, but he forestalled her. His grip on her arm was firm and she was forced to remain where she was. She dared not look up at him, as he was no doubt angry at her impertinence.

'Miss Stanton, I believe you are funning me. That is also a new experience for me, but one that I believe I could get to enjoy. Come, sweetheart, take my arm and we will walk like civilised people to collect our siblings.'

She could hardly refuse and reluctantly did as he requested. They strolled for a few yards before he spoke again. She did not dare risk her own voice, as being so close to him was giving her palpitations.

'My mother can be somewhat of a stickler, and is not famous for taking new acquaintances into her inner circle. However, today is a revelation. She has

240

taken you to her heart and is obviously enjoying the company of your uncle.' He paused, and she risked a glance in his direction to see that he was looking thoughtful.

'I like your mother, sir, and am sure that I will feel the same way about Miss Bishop and Miss Elizabeth.'

His arm tensed beneath her fingers. 'I fear that you may not. I must warn you, they can be sharp-tongued and devious. You must be very careful what you say to them, as it will be broadcast throughout the county shortly afterwards.'

Sapphire was shocked to the core and snatched her arm away from his. 'I cannot believe what I'm hearing. How can you say such things about your own sisters?'

His expression was bleak as he answered. 'I wish to be honest with you. I love my mother and my brother but find it hard to even like my sisters. They are like my father — selfish and unkind. Although they are identical twins, I honestly think they would not hesitate to betray each other if it was to their own benefit.'

There was something unsettling about these comments and she was not sure how to react. 'I am horrified that you talk of your own sisters so disparagingly. There is such a thing as family loyalty, and you obviously have none of it. I thought you someone I could like, but I was mistaken.' She stepped away from him as if he were contaminated and stalked off, making it very clear he was not welcome at her side.

Her brothers saw her approaching and ran to greet her. 'Can we go in the punt? Why is Lord Ilchester going back to the house?' David asked.

'He had forgotten there was something he had to do. You will see him this afternoon, and perhaps you can persuade him to take you out in the punt tomorrow. Remember, boys, there will be more guests arriving later and you must be on your best behaviour, or I shall banish you to your playroom.'

Gideon's sisters arrived and she could not tell them apart. This could prove awkward — but then she noticed one of them wore green ribbons and the other pink. She curtsied politely, but they merely nodded as if she was somehow beneath their notice. 'I am delighted to meet you,' Sapphire greeted them, 'and I see that you have already made the acquaintance of my siblings. Thank you for escorting them to the lake; that was kind of you.'

The young lady with pink ribbons nodded again. 'I am Emily, and this is my sister Elizabeth. I do declare, Miss Stanton, that I scarcely recognise you now that you are free of dirt and correctly dressed. We thought you a vagabond trespassing here, did we not, sister?'

'I apologise if I startled you, Miss Bishop, but I had no option in the matter. I could never leave a creature to suffer when I could do something to alleviate the problem.'

The girls exchanged glances and then Elizabeth spoke. 'A lady of decorum would not have done as you did, Miss Stanton, but have returned to the house and sent out a servant. I do hope we will not be witness to such a display again during our visit.'

Sapphire was beginning to regret her reprimand to Gideon. She had already taken a dislike to his sisters and she had only just made their acquaintance. She stared at them, her expression cold and disapproving. 'Miss Elizabeth, I believe you do not quite understand how things are. You are *my* guests and your opinion is of no matter to me or anyone else. I can make my travelling carriage available for your immediate return to Ilchester Abbey, if you are not happy here.'

The girls did not answer but flounced away, tossing their fair ringlets and muttering under their breath. David tugged her hand. 'We don't like those girls, do we, Tom? Why aren't they nice like Lord Ilchester?'

'I think that they are feeling unwell after the long journey,' said Sapphire. 'I'm sure they will be more sociable tomorrow.' This answer satisfied the boys and they trotted along beside her, chatting about this and that until Tom mentioned their nursemaid.

'Miss Bishop said that Meg didn't need to come, as they liked to look after children.'

'There — if they like to be with children, then they can't be too bad, can they?'

Somewhat reassured that Gideon's sisters were not as unpleasant as she feared, Sapphire herded the boys through the house and back to their own domain, where they would eat their lunch. They would not be allowed to eat downstairs until all the guests had departed.

Lady Serena was in the hall with her daughters and the girls were quite obviously upset. Sapphire paused, not wishing to intrude. Unfortunately Emily made no attempt to lower her voice and every word carried to the gallery.

'Mama, Miss Stanton and her brothers are quite impossible. Papa always said that having money did not make one socially acceptable. I cannot understand why Gideon has brought us here.'

'Miss Stanton is the daughter of a soldier and her brothers are the sons of a penniless clerk,' Elizabeth added, her strident tones equally audible. 'The fact that their mother was cousin to our papa does not make them acceptable. If it were not for the fact that several important families are also coming to this house party, I should wish to go home immediately.'

Sapphire had heard quite enough and was about to rush down and tell them in no uncertain terms to pack their trunks and depart forthwith, when Gideon intervened. She had not realised he had joined them, as he had been hidden beneath the gallery. His voice cut like a whip and even she flinched. 'How dare you speak so disparagingly about Miss Stanton and her brothers? Have you no manners? You are guests under this roof and will conduct yourselves accordingly. Do I make myself clear?' There was a mumbled reply from the girls which did not satisfy him. 'If you have the temerity to utter one word that could be considered uncivil or impolite, then I will have you locked in your chamber and you will remain there until I give you leave to come out. I can assure you there will be no Season for either of you if your appalling behaviour continues.'

He was quite formidable when he was angry and Sapphire almost felt sorry for his sisters. She was about to continue her descent when Lady Serena spoke out.

'Elizabeth, Emily, you will go to your room and rest. The journey has obviously disagreed with you, and if you wish to join us for dinner then you will need to recover your composure.'

Good grief! thought Sapphire. The girls were going to be on the staircase at any moment, and she would be discovered eavesdropping. Then she steadied — she would not be embarrassed or intimidated. This was her house and she could lurk or linger wherever she wished.

As it was considered unlucky to pass on the stairs, she waited politely at the top for the two young ladies to ascend. She nodded regally and to her surprise they both curtsied, and with lowered eyes they disappeared into the guest wing.

Lady Serena had gone but Gideon was waiting for her. He smiled wryly. 'I take it you heard that, and I can only apologise. I am curious to know what you said that sent them into such high alt.' He addressed her as if she had not spoken to him so harshly a short while ago.

'I told them that I could arrange to have them returned to Ilchester Abbey if they were not happy.'

'I did warn you, sweetheart, but you chose to take offence. There is no need to apologise; I'm quite happy to forgive and forget.'

He offered his arm, which she ignored; she was tempted to kick him hard in the shins instead. 'Lord Ilchester, I believe that I can say with all honesty that the only member of your family I am disposed to like is Lady Serena. I am going to eat my luncheon. You may do as you please.'

She swept past him, head held high, hoping her disdain for him was obvious. The fact that his laughter followed her did nothing for her temper.

Gideon knew he should not have laughed at her, but he had been unable to restrain himself. The more he crossed swords with Sapphire, the more determined he was to marry her. One thing was certain: life with her would never be dull.

Emily and Elizabeth had outdone themselves this time, but he would not tolerate any further impertinence. A sound spanking might rein in their excesses, but this was a task he would leave to whatever unfortunate gentle-men eventually married them.

He frowned as something occurred to him. Living under the same roof with his sisters and his future wife might well be intolerable for all of them. No matter — his mother and the girls could move into the annex. This building was a fraction of the size of the Abbey, but quite big enough for the three of them to live in comfort. When he made Sapphire an offer he must remember to make it clear she would not be obliged to share the marital home with *his* family. Instead she would have her uncle and brothers to keep her company.

He sauntered towards the small dining room and joined those already within.

'There you are, my boy,' his mother said. 'We thought you had decided to skip your midday repast.'

'I am sharp-set and have no intention of missing my meal. I think it would be unkind to make the girls go hungry,

Mama, so if you have no objection, I will ask for a tray to be sent up to them.'

Mr Bishop was already seated and tucking into a substantial plate of cold cuts, game pie and various pickles and chutneys. His niece was helping herself to the cold collation but turned and nodded approvingly.

'I have already done so, my lord, and am glad that you agree.'

He joined her at the sideboard and spoke quietly for her ears alone. 'Are we still at daggers drawn, my dear? Or shall we declare a truce?'

Her eyes narrowed and for a moment he thought his overture would be rebuffed. 'Very well, my lord, I am prepared to forget everything that has been said so far today by you and your sisters. I have no wish to begin my anniversary celebrations at odds with you.'

'On that subject, my dear, I have a gift for you. Shall I keep it until tomorrow, or would you like me to present it today?'

Her cheeks flushed becomingly and for the first time today her smile was genuine. 'I was not expecting gifts, my lord, from you or anyone else. This house party and the fête tomorrow are more than enough. I shall be twenty, which is not a significant anniversary.'

As he reached to lift a slice of succulent pink ham from a silver platter, she did the same, and their hands brushed. The contact caused her to withdraw her hand so violently that the meat on the end of her fork flew into the air and vanished over her shoulder. She clapped her hand to her mouth and spun round to see where the missing meat had gone. 'Oh dear me! I do beg your pardon, Uncle John. I cannot think how that happened.'

Mr Bishop was peeling the offending item from his sleeve. 'Never mind, Sapphire, no harm done. See, there is hardly a mark on my jacket.'

Gideon bit his lip in an attempt to keep back his amusement. He failed miserably and soon everyone was laughing. The remainder of the meal passed in high spirits. He said no more about his gift — the gold locket he had purchased for Sapphire could be presented in the morning.

14

Sir Joshua, Lady Jamieson and their two attractive daughters arrived, and Sapphire was waiting to greet them in the hall. The girls were both out and had already enjoyed one Season. They were not yet betrothed, however, which she found surprising, as they were pretty young ladies with a lively wit and pleasant manners. That they also had an impeccable pedigree and a sizeable dowry went without question.

'Lady Jamieson, Sir Joshua, welcome to Canfield Hall. Mrs Banks, our housekeeper, would be delighted to show you to your chambers, and footmen will accompany you so that you can find your way to the terrace where tea will be served when you are ready.'

Lady Jamieson, an elegant lady of middle years and faded blonde hair, shook her head. 'I thank you, Miss Stanton, but we would much rather take tea immediately. I gather Lord Ilchester and his family are already here — it will be pleasant to become reacquainted with Lady Serena and his lordship.'

That the Bishop girls were not mentioned could have been an oversight, or might have been deliberate. 'Then come this way and I shall introduce you to Mr Bishop, my great-uncle.'

Miss Jamieson dropped back to converse with Sapphire. 'Thank you so much for inviting us to your name day celebration. The countryside can be decidedly flat in the summer. We cannot wait for the next Season, as we had such a jolly time in London at all the parties, soirées and routs.'

'I am delighted you accepted the invitation, Miss Jamieson. I have not had a Season, but Uncle John is determined to rent a house in the best district for next year.'

Miss Isobel slipped her hand through Sapphire's arm. 'Will you have a ball? I do hope you do; they are such fun.' She gestured towards Gideon, who was deep in conversation with Sir Joshua. 'Your success is assured, Miss Stanton, as you will have the gentleman all debutantes have set their sights on sponsoring you. Is he not a relative of yours?'

'Indeed he is. We are second cousins, or some such thing, I believe. Would you care to walk to the lake? It is far cooler by the water than it is here on the terrace. We can have tea on our return. The Forsyths should have arrived by then.'

At the mention of this name the girls exchanged blushing smiles. 'Do their sons accompany them?' Miss Jamieson asked.

'They do, which is most fortunate as otherwise we would be sadly short of gentlemen if we wish to dance this evening. Even with them there will be a surfeit of young ladies, so we might be obliged to dance with each other.'

Her companions seemed quite happy with that suggestion and Sapphire believed she might have made a connection, and perhaps found friends of her own age for the first time in her life. The boats and boathouse were exclaimed over and then they were ready to join the others.

As they strolled back to the house, a handsome travelling coach turned into the drive, followed by two gentlemen on magnificent matching chestnut geldings. The Forsyths were arriving; they too would be far earlier than expected.

The girls could not take their gaze from the two gentlemen on horseback. 'Oh, Miss Stanton, we are so excited to meet Mr Forsyth and his brother. The county is abuzz with talk of them,' Miss Jamieson said.

'They are attractive gentlemen, and they certainly both ride well.' Sapphire's comment caused Miss Isobel to gasp.

'Attractive? They are the handsomest

men in Christendom and, although not as wealthy as Mr Bishop or titled like Lord Ilchester, there is not a single young lady who would not be ecstatic to receive an offer from one of them.'

'In which case I cannot wait to meet them myself. Having three such gentlemen in residence should make for an interesting visit.' Sapphire rather thought that Gideon might not be as pleased as her new friends at the arrival of the Forsyth brothers.

She was aware of a flutter of anticipation and felt sorry for the Bishop girls, who were banished to their bedroom. She wandered across to speak to their brother.

'My lord, I think your sisters will have understood by now that they behaved poorly. With your permission, I should like to send word to their apartment that they are at liberty to come down if they so wish.'

'If my mother is in agreement, then you may do so. It's kind of you to think of them.' He hesitated as if he wished to say more, but then merely nodded and smiled.

Lady Serena was now talking to Lady Jamieson — they were obviously bosom bows. 'Forgive me for interrupting you, but I should like to invite your daughters to join us for tea. Lord Ilchester has given his permission as long as you are happy too.'

'Are you quite sure, my dear? Much as I love my girls, I am well aware of their shortcomings, and they will not come down here sweetly smiling and contrite at their misdemeanours. They will wish to be the centre of attention and will not take kindly to anyone who stands in their way.'

If Sapphire had been startled by Gideon's condemnation of his siblings, she was even more so by their mother's plain speaking, and in front of Lady Jamieson too. She was about to comment on this extraordinary pronouncement when Lady Jamieson chuckled.

'My dear Miss Stanton, do not look

so shocked. Emily and Elizabeth are as famous throughout the county for their outrageous behaviour as they are for their outstanding beauty. When they have their come-out next year they will be at the top of any guest list, because a hostess can be assured that where they go others will follow just to see the fireworks.'

Somewhat reassured by this remark, Sapphire managed a weak smile. She had already been on the receiving end of their 'outrageous behaviour' and hoped the girls would keep themselves in check whilst residing at Canfield Hall. This was the very first anniversary party she had ever experienced and she was determined that nothing, and no one, was going to spoil it.

The new arrivals would be here any minute; she excused herself and made her way to the entrance hall in order to be there to greet them. By rights her uncle should accompany her, but he appeared to have forgotten his respon-sibilities as host. These were his friends

— he had invited them — and he really should come with her. She did not know these people and it would be embarrassing having to introduce herself.

'Miss Stanton, would you like me to accompany you?' asked Gideon, who had appeared by her side. 'I am well acquainted with Forsyth and his family and am happy to stand in your uncle's stead.'

'I would be grateful, my lord, but think it rag-mannered of him not to be here himself. I did so wish to make a favourable impression.'

His eyes glinted and he tucked her hand under his arm. 'Believe me, sweetheart, you have only to stand in front of a person to make a favourable impression.' He guided her across the terrace, down the length of the drawing room and out into the hall. Robinson and Mrs Banks were already mustering their troops — there was no need for her to be anxious, as everything was as it should be.

'I did not know the Forsyths would be attending,' said Gideon. 'They were certainly not included on my list.'

'Mr Forsyth is an old friend of my uncle's, which is why I am astonished he has not made the effort to come out to greet them.' Something mischievous prompted her to add a further comment. 'I am agog to meet Mr Forsyth's sons, for the Jamieson girls were most complimentary about them.' The arm beneath her fingers tightened and she wished her words unsaid.

'They are certainly popular with the young ladies, but have so far not shown any interest in matrimony.' He then gave an unexpected bark of laughter. 'My sisters will be first in the queue to claim them. I sincerely hope that you and the Jamieson girls are not crushed in their rush to impress.'

The front door was already standing open and two footmen were outside to lower the steps and usher these new guests inside. However, it was not Mr and Mrs Forsyth who appeared, but their sons. Sapphire caught her breath. Now she understood why Gideon had been reluctant to invite these two gentlemen and why his sisters were so eager to greet them. The first through the door had cropped fair hair, stood almost as tall as Gideon, and had the perfect features of an Adonis. His brother was close behind, slightly shorter, but broader in the shoulders and with the same colouring. They strolled towards her and she could sense her companion almost quivering with dislike.

'Good grief, Ilchester, I might have known you would be here first and stake your claim on the most beautiful young lady in the county.' The speaker bowed low. 'I am Rupert Forsyth and this is my younger brother, Richard. Thank you for inviting us to your house party, Miss Stanton.'

Sapphire curtsied. 'I am delighted that you could come. There will be tea on the terrace when you are ready.' They took the hint; she rather thought they had intended to join the party smelling of the stable. They sauntered away with the housekeeper, promising to return as soon as they were changed.

What was keeping Mr and Mrs Forsyth outside so long? 'Robinson, is anything amiss out there?' Sapphire asked the butler, who was standing guard at the top of the steps.

'No, miss. Your little brothers have their puppy and are speaking with Mr and Mrs Forsyth.'

'In which case, I shall go out and introduce myself and not wait here.' She smiled at Gideon. 'There is no need for you to accompany me, thank you, unless you wish to.'

He shrugged as if not bothered either way. 'In which case, my dear, I shall return to the terrace. I think you are wise to join the Forsyths outside, as I am certain I can hear my sisters approaching.' His disarming smile robbed the words of any censor.

Silly was yapping and dancing around the boys like a whirligig, much to the visitors' amusement. Sapphire picked up her skirts and ran lightly down the steps to greet them. David saw her coming and rushed to meet her.

'We are being good, Saffy, but Silly got out of the loose box and we had to come after him.'

'Where is Meg? You should be with her, not running about on your own.'

Mrs Forsyth came over, smiling broadly. 'My dear Miss Stanton, I do beg your pardon for dallying out here with your charming brothers and their delightful puppy. I am Mrs Forsyth and this is my husband. We were so glad to hear from Mr Bishop and to receive his invitation to join you for this prestigious event.' She barely paused for breath before continuing. 'I suppose my naughty boys have already made themselves welcome. We were so surprised they wished to accompany us — usually they are about their own business. They have their own estates, you know; they do not dwell with us anymore.'

Sapphire was reeling under the weight of words. Mr Forsyth raised an eyebrow and then strolled over to join them. He half-bowed and she dipped in a small curtsy. 'I am pleased to make the acquaintance of you and your brothers, Miss Stanton.' He gripped his wife's arm firmly. 'Come along, my dear, we must find our accommodations and refresh ourselves before meeting the rest of the guests.'

The nursemaid arrived looking guilty, and hastily gathered up her errant charges. The girl was spending far too much time in the stable yard — was it possible she was forming an attachment to Billy? There was no time to dwell on this possibility as there were duties to perform.

'My housekeeper will take you to your apartment, Mrs Forsyth,' Sapphire told him, 'and a footman will bring you to the terrace, where we are gathered drinking tea and eating cake.'

The last arrivals disappeared up the grand staircase, leaving her to catch her breath before returning to her guests. As she stepped into the drawing room, she could see the assembled company milling around outside the French doors. Canfield Hall had never been so lively or so elegant. She was ready to play the hostess, and prayed that nothing untoward would take place over the next few days.

The four young ladies were tweeting and trilling around the handsome brothers, who were obviously enjoying the attention. Uncle John appeared to be asleep and Gideon was sitting on the stone balustrade surveying the party. There was something vaguely proprietorial about his manner and this set her teeth on edge.

She decided to join him, but not before she had checked that her dearest uncle was comfortable. She was heading in his direction when Gideon intercepted her.

'He is asleep, sweetheart. I was with him but a moment ago. Everything is going swimmingly, don't you think? Do you care to stroll around the garden with me?'

'I should love to, but must remain here in case I am needed by my guests. Mr and Mrs Forsyth will be down soon and it would be impolite not to be here to introduce them.'

'They are well acquainted with the company; indeed, my love, everybody here is known to each other. I should leave them to their own devices and walk with me.'

He was irresistible when he put his mind to it and her earlier irritation was forgotten. 'Actually, my lord, I should like to walk round to the meadow where Sultan and Starlight are grazing.'

The sun was warm on Sapphire's face and the sky was cloudless. This boded well for the garden party tomorrow. They walked companionably, neither feeling the need to speak. Then she recalled the garrulous Mrs Forsyth. 'I am not surprised that Uncle John did not visit with the Forsyths. Although Mrs Forsyth is quite charming, she is rather overwhelming.'

'Exactly so, sweetheart. It's a small wonder their sons vacated the familial home as soon as they could.'

She stopped and fixed him with her sternest look. 'Lord Ilchester, I have spoken to you on this subject before and you have chosen to ignore me. Kindly do not lard your conversation with unwanted and unnecessary endearments — I have no wish to give my guests an erroneous impression of our relationship.'

They were screened from both the house and the stable yard by a convenient hedge, and this was the ideal place to have an intimate conversation. To Sapphire's consternation, instead of answering her, Gideon stepped closer. Too close — his chest was almost touching hers. There was no where she could go to escape, as his bulk was trapping her against the hedge.

'Please, my lord, this is most unseemly . . . ' She was unable to continue as he reached out and gently cupped her face. The feel of his fingers against her cheek made her knees tremble.

'You mentioned our relationship, my darling, and you know as well as I do how things stand between us.'

Before she could think of a sensible reply she was in his arms, and her world tilted as his lips brushed across hers. She should protest. She should be pushing him away, but instead she pressed closer, giddy with excitement. Her feet left the ground and he kissed her for a second time, his mouth hard against hers. She buried her fingers in his hair and was transported to a place no unmarried girl should go.

With a sigh he slid her down his body until her feet were once more on the ground. 'Now, I think you understand the situation. Shall I go down on one knee here, or would you prefer that we found somewhere a little more romantic?'

If he had not been holding her

elbows she would have collapsed in a heap at his feet. She closed her eyes and leaned back into the prickly privet behind her. Maybe if he released her arms she would be able to think coherently; with him so close her heart continued to thunder as if intending to escape from the confines of her bodice.

As if divining her thoughts, his hands moved from her elbows, down her forearms and stopped when he held her hand in his. 'Sapphire, look at me. God's teeth! Have I mistaken your feelings?' His expletive shocked her to her senses. She straightened and opened her eyes to find him still disconcertingly close. 'I love you and I want to marry you. Please tell me that you feel the same.'

For the first time since she'd met him he sounded unsure. She gazed up into his face and what she saw there made everything clear. 'I do believe I feel the same. I had not fully understood how much you meant to me until now.'

His eyes blazed with triumph and he

was about to drop to his knee to propose formally when she stopped him. 'Please, do not say it. I cannot marry you, as I cannot leave my uncle.'

'I have it all worked out, darling girl. You will all come to live at Ilchester Abbey and I shall put tenants here until your brothers are of age.'

'I don't think you understand what I'm trying to tell you, my lord. I have no wish to live anywhere but at Canfield Hall. Why don't you and your family come to live here instead?'

His expression changed as if she had struck him across the face. 'Come here? That is not how it works, Sapphire. When a young lady marries she must go where her husband directs. If you are concerned that my sisters would be a constant source of friction, then fear not; that too can be smoothed over by moving them to the annex.'

The rose-tinted spectacles fell from her eyes and she finally understood the reason behind her hesitation. 'If that be the case, sir, then I am glad you have not made me a formal offer, for my answer would have been no. As we were quite unobserved when we misbehaved then I am in no way compromised by your actions. However, I must insist that in future you keep your distance and address me as if I were a stranger.'

He appeared stunned by her rejection, and she took the opportunity to slip away before he could continue his persuasion. There was no doubt that she loved this autocratic, irritating, high-handed aristocrat, but apparently not enough to wish to leave Canfield Hall.

15

Gideon watched the infuriating girl scurry away. Sapphire would be certain she had resolved matters in her favour and that he would follow her every dictum to the letter. This house party was going to be even more interesting than he had expected, but by the end of it he was determined to change her mind. He would be engaged to Miss Sapphire Stanton and she would be as delighted as he was at the prospect.

However, tonight he would allay her suspicions by doing as she'd asked and ignoring her. If he danced with everyone but her, she might feel a twinge of jealousy and begin to reconsider her decision. He strode in through the front door and rejoined the noisy group on the terrace.

His eyes narrowed when he saw his future wife engaged in conversation with one of the Forsyth gentlemen. It took considerable restraint to ignore this provocation, but intervening would not help his cause. Then he relaxed. Whatever his beloved said to the contrary, he knew she returned his love and would not be interested in anyone else.

His sisters were looking daggers and this did not bode well. He had better defuse the situation before it escalated. 'Elizabeth, Emily, I trust you are fully recovered from your earlier indisposition?'

His tone was bland but his siblings understood the message hidden beneath his words. Elizabeth smiled sunnily. 'We are indeed, brother, and thank you kindly for asking. We can assure you there will be no recurrence of the 'indisposition' that required us to retire to our chamber.'

Emily managed a weak smile, but her eyes were still firmly fixed on the couple standing by the tea table. 'Miss Stanton is not yet out. Shall we be presented together next Season? After all, Mama is most suited to sponsoring her, don't you think, Gideon?'

What game was his sister playing now? 'The fact that Miss Stanton has not appeared at court or in London does not mean that she is not out. Remember, Emily, that she runs this vast household and is hostess for this grand occasion. Not every young lady wishes to be the belle of the ball and spend several months being crushed at a variety of prestigious venues in town.'

He had both girls' full attention now — they were staring at him as if he had been speaking in tongues. Eventually Elizabeth replied. 'Not wish to attend a ball? I can scarcely believe it.' She turned to her sister, who was equally perplexed. 'If Miss Stanton does not like to dance, that surely means she will wish to sit with the matrons tonight.'

This was not what he had meant at all, but he would be happy if Sapphire didn't dance; the thought of her in the arms of any other gentleman but him was not a pleasant one. He was about to retire to the library when his mother drifted up to his side.

'Gideon, I wish to speak to you most urgently. Shall we go inside where we will be private?'

Once they were well away from the open doors she stared at him most earnestly. 'I know what you are about. I suspected it from the start, and now that I see you together I am certain.'

'What do you suspect me of, Mama? I'm intrigued to know.' His stock felt unaccountably tight and he resisted the urge to run his finger round it.

'Do not bandy words with me, my boy. You have decided to marry Miss Stanton and you had us included in your invitation here as camouflage for your intentions. No, there is no need to deny it. I have seen the way you look at her and she at you — and I can assure you that you have my full approval.'

There was little point in denying the truth. '*Mea culpa*, Mama. I was smitten the moment I saw her and, despite being constantly at daggers drawn, every moment I have spent in her company has served to reinforce my opinion.'

'I take it from the fact that she is studiously ignoring you means your suit has not prospered. Gideon, she only discovered her uncle a few months ago; she will not be ready to abandon him so soon. Why are you in such a pother to tie the knot? I'm sure that next year she will receive your attentions with more favour.'

'I am not a nincompoop, Mama; I have no intention of separating her from Mr Bishop. I explained to her that they could all come and live at the Abbey — there is more than enough room.'

His mother looked unconvinced by his logic. 'My dear boy, do you honestly think that the girls and a new bride are compatible?'

'I have thought of that as well. I shall move you and the girls into the annex — there is ample space for the three of you — and then we can have the Abbey to ourselves.'

'Shall you indeed? I for one will be quite content living in restricted accommodation, but I can assure you your sisters will not. So let us pray they find themselves suitable husbands next Season and thus remove the problem.' She patted him on the arm. 'I think it would be wise to leave your own nuptials until after your sisters are spoken for. You are more likely to convince Miss Stanton that she wishes to be your wife if you take your time courting her.'

His eyes darkened. It was preposterous to even consider changing his plans in order to accommodate the whims of his spoilt sisters. If they behaved badly they would discover he would not tolerate disobedience and that he was not to be trifled with.

He needed some fresh air before he was obliged to change for dinner. As he turned to leave he caught a flash of green ribbon, and his chest squeezed as if he had swallowed a large stone. Elizabeth had been lurking in the corner of the drawing room and could have overheard his conversation.

★ ★ ★

Sapphire was running late and would barely have time to change and dress her hair. She had been called to the nursery when Thomas had cast up his accounts. Her brother was now sleeping and David appeared not to have been plagued by the same unpleasant problem.

Jenny was waiting for her. 'Quickly, miss, I heard a carriage just now.'

They managed her transformation in just over a quarter of an hour, and when Sapphire viewed herself in the full-length mirror she was delighted with her appearance. 'With these long gloves on the scratches do not show, and the ringlets on either side of my face cleverly disguise the other damage. Thank you, I believe that I am ready to go down. I sincerely hope my uncle was there to greet whichever guests arrived. He was most insistent we invite all the neighbours that are within driving distance to dine tonight, and this will make thirty guests.'

She all but ran along the spacious passageway and down the grand staircase. There was no sign of her uncle or the early arrivals, but Lord Ilchester was waiting for her. He bowed politely.

'Mr Bishop is with your guests, and he has requested that I remain here with you to welcome the others who are expected.' He did not sound especially delighted to be given this task.

'That is typical of Uncle John. I have no idea who is expected and will not know one from the other.'

'Which is why, Miss Stanton, I am to stand with you so that I might introduce you. Mr Bishop has invited those on my list and is not acquainted with them either.'

There were voices coming from above and she looked up to see Lady

Serena and her daughters descending. Serena was magnificent in burgundy, the matching turban ablaze with jewels and egret feathers. Elizabeth and Emily were wearing white, as was usual with debutantes, and Sapphire's own gold silk gown now seemed inappropriate.

'My lord, as the strangers who are attending tonight are your friends and not mine, then I shall leave you and Lady Serena to greet them in my stead.' Sapphire dipped politely to Serena and ignored the sisters, and before Gideon could protest she abandoned him. If her uncle thought it perfectly proper for Lord Ilchester to act as host then so be it — but she was not going to remain there with him. Having him beside her, introducing her to his friends, would give the erroneous impression that she was something she was not. Small wonder he had agreed or that her uncle had suggested it. They were both doing their best to manipulate her into the betrothal she had no wish for.

She circulated amongst the elegant

people gathered in the drawing room, but one face blurred into another and she knew she could not recall a single name if required to do so. What had possessed her to agree to this nonsense? Entertaining a room full of someone else's friends was a recipe for disaster.

When Robinson appeared at the door to announce that dinner was served, she had expected to lead the procession with her uncle. However, those nearest the door followed the butler, leaving her to find her own way in. Then she felt a firm grip on her elbow.

'That was poorly done of you, Miss Stanton,' Gideon told her. 'You are now labelled as either uncivil or eccentric by those who were not greeted by you this evening.'

'I care not. They are your friends, not mine. The sooner this farce is over the happier I shall be. I have no wish to be escorted by you, sir; I am quite capable of finding my way into my own dining room.'

Instead of releasing her, his fingers

tightened. 'You will walk beside me and behave yourself, young lady, whatever your personal feelings on the matter. I will not have you embarrassing your uncle any further.'

Short of having an unseemly struggle, she had no choice but to acquiesce to his demand. This was another black mark to add to his tally: not only was he arrogant and toplofty, but also dictatorial.

Despite the unseemly rush, Robinson somehow maintained his dignity, and the company were seating themselves in an orderly fashion. John was at the head of the table with Serena beside him, while Sapphire was firmly guided to the other end of the table where two chairs had been left vacant. She had no option but to allow herself to be placed next to his lordship. The expression on her uncle's face showed that he had achieved his objective, and made it perfectly clear to the assembled guests that Ilchester had staked his claim and received his approval.

Dinner was interminable and Sapphire scarcely tasted any of the delicious food placed in front of her. She did her best to appear happy with the *fait accompli* and smiled and nodded when spoken to by Ilchester or anyone else. However, she was seething inside and determined to do something so outrageous that even Ilchester would not wish to continue his pursuit.

At one point she became aware she was receiving several less-than-favourable glances from the matrons in the party — no doubt her appalling manners earlier had not gone down well. She regretted the impulse that had driven her from the entrance hall — whatever her personal feelings, she knew better than to behave like a spoilt brat. Her incivility had, as Ilchester had so kindly pointed out, caused her uncle embarrassment. She must put aside her personal feelings for the moment and do her best to retrieve the situation.

Eventually the meal was finished and she smiled around the table and slowly stood up. This was the signal for the ladies to depart and leave the gentlemen to their port. Two footmen opened the double doors that led back into the drawing room, and she ushered her guests ahead of her.

'The night is warm. Perhaps it would be more pleasant to sit on the terrace than remain inside. I have asked for the carpet to be rolled up in the saloon and will be happy to play later on for those who wish to dance.'

This announcement provoked a murmur of approval from the young ladies, but she would have to do more to retrieve her reputation with the matrons. She spent the next half an hour circulating and apologising for her absence — she offered no excuse as there was none. By the time the gentlemen appeared she was confident she had restored her reputation somewhat.

The Bishop girls approached. One of them smiled — Sapphire had no idea which — whilst the other waited beside her sister. 'Miss Stanton, do you really intend to play for us? Do you not wish to dance yourself?'

'You will be astounded to hear it, Miss Bishop, but I am not proficient at dancing. I should much prefer to play the pianoforte than make a cake of myself on the dance floor. If you and your sister would care to come to the saloon you can choose suitable music for me to play — there is a prodigious amount in the cabinet and I have no notion which would be best.'

The girls were being remarkably pleasant and not at all as she had expected. Possibly the fact that there was to be dancing, and one less unattached young lady looking for a partner, had softened their opinion. Within a short space of time half a dozen sheets of music had been selected.

'Can you sight-read, Miss Stanton? Are you ready to play or would you like a while to practise?'

Sapphire examined each piece in

turn. 'They are all straightforward. I should have no difficulty. If you would care to fetch those who would like to dance, I shall run through the first. This one, I believe, is for the country dance.'

The two ran off at once to summon the younger set. Sapphire did a rapid calculation in her head and, if she was not mistaken, there were five single gentlemen and seven young ladies. The country dances needed five couples so this would be ideal to open the proceedings.

She had the music for a cotillion, a quadrille and a reel. The Bishop girls had assured her there would be several amongst the party who could do the intricate steps that were required in the reel when the music paused. Although all the young ladies apart from the Bishop girls were out, Sapphire had no intention of playing the tune for the waltz. This risky dance had become popular but would not be approved of by the matrons, and she had offended them sufficiently for one evening.

After an hour of playing lively tunes she was ready for a respite, but did not have the heart to stop as everyone was having such fun. Then a familiar voice spoke from behind her. 'You play beautifully, Miss Stanton, but you have more than made up for your inauspicious start to the evening.' Lord Ilchester reached over her shoulder and carefully closed the piano. 'Enough. If they wish to dance, they must find someone amongst themselves to provide the music.' He placed his hand gently under her elbow and guided her to her feet. He looked remarkably unflushed for a gentleman who had been skipping around the dance floor for the past hour.

'Were you not dancing, my lord? I would have thought you in high demand.'

'The only partner I wish to have was otherwise engaged.'

She wished he would not say things like that. He was putting intolerable pressure on her to accept his offer, and she was certain being married to him would be a disaster. He was not a biddable gentleman; he would take charge of everything and leave no decisions to her.

They strolled the length of the saloon, across the drawing room and out into the cool summer evening. He walked her to the far end of the terrace, away from those who had chosen to sit outside. Although the nightingales no longer sang, there were blackbirds and thrushes filling the air with glorious sound. There could be nowhere as beautiful or pleasant as Canfield Hall. Sapphire was sure that although she had feelings for the man standing beside her, they were not strong enough to compensate for what she would lose if she moved away. Matters would be quite different if Uncle John was no longer with them but, God willing, that day was a long time in the future. One thing she was sure of: Ilchester would not be prepared to wait for her.

'Thank you for rescuing me, sir. I

would much prefer to be outside than in the saloon playing the pianoforte.'

He appeared to be in no hurry to either release her arm or reply to her remark. He had brought her out here, so why was he ignoring her? There was something she wished to say that would definitely get his attention, but first she must remove herself a distance away.

When she was a few yards from him she thought it safe to say what was on her mind. 'I know what you and my uncle are about, my lord. You have made it abundantly clear to all the important families in the county that if we are not actually betrothed, the announcement will come in due course.' She waited for his reaction but he remained motionless, gazing out across the park as if uninterested in her views.

'I might be prepared to consider marrying, but not now, not whilst my uncle is alive. Unless you are prepared to live here with me, then I cannot agree to become your wife in the foreseeable future.'

His reaction was infuriating; he laughed as if at the ramblings of an amusing child. 'Do you think, my darling girl, that you will escape me quite so easily? I have spoken with Mr Bishop, my mother and sisters, and they are all in agreement — I have made the perfect choice and they cannot wait to see us conjoined.'

This was the outside of enough. How dare he discuss her with his sisters? Whatever her treacherous uncle wished, she would not marry Ilchester, but would remain a spinster until circumstances at Canfield Hall changed. 'I care not what your family think on the subject, sir. The decision is mine and I shall not change my mind.' She did not remain to hear his reply but dashed in unseemly haste to join her guests.

16

The tea tray was brought in shortly after Sapphire arrived and she performed her duties impeccably. Uncle John had already retired, but he had the excuse of failing health and nobody was upset by his desertion. No one else had offered to play the piano so there had been no further dancing.

Lady Serena came to sit with Sapphire on the chaise longue. 'I gather you have employed musicians for tomorrow night's entertainment, Miss Stanton. It was kind of you to forego the pleasure of dancing yourself in order to allow others to dance this evening.'

'I do not enjoy dancing. I know that is tantamount to sacrilege, but I much prefer to play or listen than participate.'

'How quaint! My son did not dance either, and this omission was noted, I can assure you.' The lady gave an arch smile. 'Although nothing has been said officially, I am delighted that you will soon be joining us at the Abbey. Do not look so worried, my dear. The girls and I will remove ourselves to the annex so that you might be private with your own family.'

Sapphire's horrified expression was caused because Lady Serena had a carrying voice and all in the vicinity would have heard her comment. She was torn — should she make the circumstances clear and risk offending Lady Serena, or accept the inevitable?

'I'm afraid you are a little premature in your assumptions, my lady. Although we do have an understanding, I will not be joining you at the Abbey.'

Instead of being taken aback by this remark, her ladyship nodded and smiled. 'Of course — how kind of my son to think of us like that. He will come and live here with you at Canfield Hall and thus allow my daughters and me to remain at the Abbey and not be obliged to squeeze into the inferior accommodation of the annex.'

Lady Jamieson wandered over to join them. 'Did I hear correctly? Are you and Lord Ilchester to announce your betrothal tomorrow at your anniversary party? How exciting — we did wonder why you were arranging such an elaborate event, and now we understand.'

The cup and saucer in Sapphire's hand rattled and she was obliged to put them down. This was an unmitigated disaster, and it was all of her own doing. She must find Gideon and explain what had transpired before he was congratulated on his forthcoming nuptials by somebody else.

She politely excused herself and began her search. He wasn't with the other gentlemen, or in the saloon with the younger members of the group, and neither was he striding up and down the terrace. Where could he be at this time of night?

She slipped back into the hall and

found Robinson on duty. 'Do you have any idea of the whereabouts of Lord Ilchester?'

'He has gone to the lake, Miss Stanton. He asked me to leave the side door unbolted so he could return when he wished and not keep anyone up.'

Why on earth would he wish to go there in the middle of the night? Her heeled evening slippers would be quite ruined if she ventured out into the dew-damp grass with them on. She had said goodnight to her guests so they would assume she had retired; however, she had no intention of doing so until she had spoken to Gideon.

She left by the side door and immediately leant against the wall to remove her shoes and stockings. If she draped her skirts over her arm she was certain she could keep them from the damp. She would hate to ruin this gown, as it was one of her favourites.

Fortunately the evening was clement and there was no need for her to worry about fetching a wrap from inside.

Although the moon was a mere sliver in the sky, there was sufficient illumination for her to pick her way slowly across the grass, but she did not see her quarry until she was almost at the water's edge. Gideon was standing waiting for her. Her heart skipped a beat and she wondered if she had been entirely wise coming down here alone in the dark when he was so determined to persuade her to marry him. The thought of what persuasion he might employ sent an unaccustomed wave of heat to a most unexpected place and she almost dropped her skirts in surprise.

'Good evening, my love. You have taken an unconscionable time to reach me. I think a snail might have traversed the distance with more speed than you did.'

'I could not come any faster as the grass is far lumpier than I expected, and I had difficulty holding up my skirt and keeping my balance.'

He stepped forward and glanced down. 'Devil take it! What possessed you to come over here in bare feet?'

'I could not wear my slippers as they would have been ruined by the dew.' She noticed he had changed into his boating clothes and was also without his shoes and socks. 'What are you doing here, and why did you ask Robinson to leave the door open for you? Do you intend to stay out all night?'

He gestured towards the rowing boat pulled up against the jetty. 'I thought I would try and catch one of the magnificent carp you have swimming in this lake, and fishing is better done at night.'

This was a strange conversation to be having after what had taken place between them earlier that evening. 'I had no idea there were fish, for I have never seen them. Anyway, that's as may be, my lord. I wish to speak to you about something.'

'I rather gathered that you did, sweetheart, or you would not have trekked across here to see me. Just a moment — I have the very thing for you.' He reached into the depths of the boat and removed a large blanket, which he promptly enveloped her in. Before she could wriggle free he had swept her up and deposited her on the padded seat at the rear of the boat.

He then stepped nimbly in, folded himself onto the central plank, and took up the oars. It would be fruitless to protest; she was being taken for a ride whether she wished it or not. She settled back, cosy and warm within the folds of the blanket, and closed her eyes, enjoying the gentle rocking sensation.

The whisper of the water as it passed the hull and the creak of the oars as they moved were the only sounds in the darkness; then Sapphire heard a nightjar calling and the cough of a pheasant in the woods. This would not do — it was all very well for him to abduct her in this way, but she had come to tell him of the disaster she had precipitated.

'I have been speaking to your mama

and one thing led to another,' she said. 'Somehow I gave her the erroneous impression we intended to be married and that you were going to move here. She was delighted you were being so considerate of her feelings. Then Lady Jamieson overheard, and no doubt the entire party is now expecting us to announce our betrothal tomorrow.'

He stopped rowing and very slowly brought the oars on board. Then he moved with catlike grace to join her on the seat. 'And how did she get the impression that I intended to abandon the Abbey and make my home at Canfield Hall?'

She had shifted as far as she could on the seat but somehow his thigh was still touching hers — even with the thickness of the blanket and her skirts she was aware it was there. She swallowed, and her voice emerged as little more than a whisper. 'I told Lady Serena I would not be living at the Abbey and she misinterpreted my comment.'

Somehow his arm had insinuated itself around her waist and the restraining folds of the blanket were now around her feet. 'Do you love me, Sapphire Stanton?' He breathed the words into her ear and her head spun with excitement.

'I do, but — '

'There are no buts, my darling. If Mohammed will not go to the mountain . . . '

'I have no idea what you're talking about — what have mountains and prophets to do with the situation?'

'If you will not come to the Abbey then I must come to Canfield Hall. If I am honest, I would much prefer to make my home here. The Abbey is ancient and hideously uncomfortable, and I have not lived there since I reached my majority.'

If he had sprung wings and flown into the sky she could not have been more surprised. Quite forgetting she was in an unstable rowing boat, she jumped to her feet. The next thing she knew she was tumbling backwards with a despairing cry, and Gideon had no option but to follow. The water was more than two yards deep out here in the middle and dangerously full of weeds. He dived in and swam strongly in the direction he believed she had gone. Even with his eyes open it was impossible to see and he was forced to grope blindly, praying his fingers would grasp her skirts. His lungs were bursting and still he had not found her. He shot to the surface, intending to take a gulp of air and then return.

'There you are, my lord. I was about to come in search of you, for you have been immersed so long.'

He clutched at the side of the rowing boat and stared in disbelief into the face of his beloved, who was sitting, admittedly drenched to the skin, quite happily in the boat and laughing down at him.

'I'm tempted to tip you in again, young lady, for giving me such a scare. I thought you had drowned.'

She moved to the far side of the boat, thus allowing him to roll over the side and join her. 'I was somewhat startled to fall in, but I am an expert swimmer if you recall, and was in no danger. However, I am suitably appreciative of your efforts on my behalf.' Her smile melted his anger. 'I also most humbly apologise for causing the accident. I quite forgot we were afloat.' Then to his astonishment she stood gracefully, this time keeping her balance, and began to remove her garments.

'What the devil are you doing? Please, you must not . . . I cannot . . . ' He was reduced to mumbling like a lovesick boy.

Instead of being shocked, she laughed and her dress and petticoats joined the blanket in the well of the boat. She stood in her chemise, which clung like a second skin to her womanly curves, and dived, with more elegance than he had, into the lake.

Without a second thought he joined her, and for a glorious half-hour they frolicked and swam like two children.

'Shall we push the boat back to shore, my love?' suggested Gideon. 'And then we must find something with which to dry ourselves.'

When the boat bumped against the jetty he was out of the water before her, and then leaned down to hoist her out. Her teeth were chattering; this midnight swim had not been a sensible idea.

'Could you please pass me the blanket from the boat?' she asked. 'I am half-frozen.'

There was another way they could get warm, and seeing her with the silvery light outlining her breasts and hips, he knew he was in danger of pre-empting their wedding night.

He turned his back to hide his embarrassment and hastily grabbed the blanket. 'Here, sweetheart, wrap yourself in that and then go back to the house. It would not do for us to be seen so dishevelled together.' He ached to take her in his arms and show her just how much he loved her, but now was not the time, and the boathouse was certainly not the place.

When she was safely cocooned inside the blanket she came closer, and one bare arm slipped out from the folds to rest lightly on his cheek. 'I love you, Gideon, and will be happy to marry you whenever you wish.'

He reached out to take her in his arms but she skipped away. 'Then we will announce it tomorrow and be married in September,' he said. His heart was bursting with happiness. 'That will give me time to refurbish the Abbey.'

Her laughter carried back to him as she vanished across the grass. 'There is no need to do that, for we have agreed that we will be living here.'

He shot after her and caught her easily. He crushed her against his chest and she turned her face up to receive his kiss. Minutes later he raised his head and looked down at the woman who would be his wife very soon. 'I don't give a damn where we live as long as we are together.'

Her smile was radiant. 'And neither do I, my love. Tonight I have learned my true feelings. I will marry you and live wherever you please.'

With a shout of triumph that sent a flock of roosting pigeons clattering into the air in protest, he spun her round. 'That is all I wished to hear. I know we will be happy anywhere as long as we are together.'